Toyco Publishing Presents

HOOD GAMES II

Tony & The Clique Reunited

I0641198

A Novel By

TOYLIN SIMONE

I Dedicate this Book to God

Through You all things are Possible.

My Beautiful Grandmother

Doris "Dottie" Bye

I Love You Forever & Ever

R.I.P.

Acknowledgements

My beautiful kids Taliya, Jordan, and Fendi, you are my everything. My motivation, my drive, you changed my life and everything I do is for you love Mom xoxo. My beautiful sisters NIKA & TEQUAN & My Sister Friend NIKKI. There is no stronger bond or love like your sisters xoxo. Tracy Ferguson love you and thank you for being a real sister/friend xoxo. Crystal/ Crysp Billz love you much Billzie xoxo. Baisley, 40p, SSJQ QGTM xoxo. Troy Casey Love You 4life. Marcella Casey xoxo. My Day One Sadaya I love you 4life xoxo. Michele Tompkins- Hines love you beautiful you are a genuine soul keep rising xoxo. To All Friends and family who have supported my movement thus far thank you xoxo. R.I.P. to my great uncle Melvin. Love you uncle Melvin xoxo. All the hustlers and go getters, keep grinding, working hard and striving for greatness. Creativity and talent is a great gift.

Stay Focused! Marques & Ebony! Sundeee What's Poppin Stay Fly xoxo. Playwright Author Amonty- Thank you for being a great inspiration and a dear friend you are awesome and super talented I wish you nothing but prosperity and success. Louis Valentine- FACES of Hip Hop much love and success. The greatest artist worldwide history. Shante Lashy & MiMi- (Eyelash Vizion) You are a great inspiration love you ladies. Keep rising, keep grinding & keep on smiling...

South Side Jamaica Queens Stand Up!

Thankful for my Strength and Courage to

Write God is so Good Blessed...

The Journey

When your magnitude of thinking differs from others you become the creator of your own world. There are many people who are chosen for this position. Only the strong survive the tasks to make it last full throttle. To make it in any setting, you must be ready to weather any storm, stand tall in the rain and overcome all struggles through the pain. It takes a courageous being to overcome rough roads, hurdle obstacles and circumstance. The rewards you receive and gain during the process are priceless. Never give up on yourself and always trust your instincts. Your soul is your ultimate backbone. What you feed it determines every outcome. The lessons in every journey paves the way to your destiny.

If you can hurdle every obstacle with an opened mind; you are more than well on your way. Confidence is beautiful. Give yourself a chance to be great. Train your mind to see the good in every situation. Be a risk taker. You are the only one that can ever hold you back. If something scares you, you should try it. Change is always a great thing. Move forward with pride and detach yourself from anyone who hinders your spirit and growth. The Journey is yours. Rise up, grind hard, stay motivated and humble peace…

PROLOGUE

The Heist

"Listen, let's just run in there, do what we gotta do and get the fuck up out of there. Frederico got a few men coming through as we speak. There is a teller who works there named Annessa'. She's going to be behind the window at the front desk. She sits directly near the vault with all the cash. Once we get inside, there's no turning back. Make sure you keep your eyes open at all times."

Clay' explained the measures of the bank job inside of a dark blue van with tinted windows to his man Tony and two other assailants before heading inside to rob it. "Look, it's about to be a hostage situation if anything goes left. I'm not going back to jail. I'm not going back to the pen.

I'd rather die than to go back. If anything happens in there, I'm going all out. It's kill or be killed fuck that." "Tony let his partner know that he was down for whatever and he was ready to get rich or die trying. Walking into the bank, there were three different tellers with a few people waiting on each line. Standing on the line, Tony looked up and noticed two cameras pointed in the direction of the entrance near the security guard.

He had on a pair of shades and a black hoodie and had a black stocking cap up under his hoodie ready to set shit off. He looked around the bank and quickly noticed the teller his man described inside of the van before they walked in. Annessa was sitting behind the window at her station talking to a potential customer like she said she would be.

She knew everything that was about to go down and agreed to play along with the robbery taken place. She disclosed all info of the security guards who were on shift that morning. She also had complete access to all camera recordings and shut them off for the day. Annessa gave a full and accurate description of each vault that had money in it.

She also included the time of one of the security guard's thirty-minute break and the exact time he usually returned into the bank. Tony's partner Clay watched him from a distance as he stood on the line; then he signaled him to make his move as he walked up to the teller. "Welcome to National Savings Bank. How may I help you?" The bank teller at the front desk greeted the gentleman who stood before her on the line.

The gentleman approached her in full speed placing a pistol into her face. "Don't you move bitch, or I'll blow your mother fucking head off." The bank teller was frightened as she listened to everything the gunman asked of her. "Everybody get on the fucking floor now." Tony shouted. Waving his gun in the air. "Listen up, this is a bank robbery. We are robbing this bank. Now, you can comply and live, or you can resist and die.

The choice is yours. I suggest you comply comfortably, so you can get back home to your families safely. The four gunmen were robbing the bank in broad day light. "We got about six minutes to empty out the vaults." Clay mentioned. Pointing his gun at the teller who sat on the floor near the front desk.

One of the teller's behind the window, placed her hand on the button to signal the silent alarm. "I said don't move, stupid mother fucker." Clay walked up to the teller and smacked her in the face with the butt of his gun.

The loud cries rang throughout the bank as the teller sobbed in agony, bloody faced and hurt by the blow to her head. The security guard who lay on the floor thought of reaching for his pistol as the tellers leaned against the wall on the floor while Tony tied their hands and feet up along with their co-workers and lined them up behind the counter near the vault. "Not so fast." Clay whispered. Grabbing the gun out of the security guard's hand. The silent alarm that the teller pressed, alerted the National Police Station.

"We got a possible robbery attempt at National Savings Bank. I repeat, we got a possible robbery attempt at National Savings Bank. I need two units down there right now." The dispatcher at the police department alerted the police officers on duty and gave them the location of the robbery. "Please don't kill us. You can take whatever you want. I have a family at home. I have two daughters who are waiting for me to pick them up from school."

The Caucasian women pleaded with the robber begging him not to take the lives of her and her co-workers. "Put the money in the bag and shut the fuck up. You think I give a fuck about you and your family right now? Say another word and I will blow your head off."

Tony looked at the lady who was crying with disgust.

All gunmen had four large bags filled with cash. "Come on that's enough. Don't be too greedy. That's enough let's go." Clay hollered. Pointing his gun at the customers lying on the floor. Tony ignored every word and proceeded to take more money filling up a fifth bag. As Tony filled the extra bag, he could hear the loud sirens approaching the bank.

"Come on we gotta get the fuck out of here right now." Looking out the window, Clay could see two police cars in front of the bank. He quickly grabbed one of the tellers who worked at the bank and demanded her to escort him and his crew to another exit. Running through the bank, Clay grabbed the woman's hair swinging her body as they made a run from the police.

The teller pointed to the exit and cried covering her face with her hands. Clay shoved the woman to the floor and proceeded to open the door. "Freeze! Don't move mother fucker. The police officer shouted. Standing in the back exit of the bank pointing a pistol at Clay's face. Both gunmen looked at one another and put their hands in the air…

Two Months Earlier...

CHAPTER 1

THE CLIQUE

Mona stepped into the shower with ease. Her mood was especially good this morning as she lathered her wash cloth with Olay body wash. Calm thoughts entered her head as the warm water hit her face running down her chin hitting her firm breasts. Mona just smiled thinking about the amazing night she had a few nights ago with a good friend. She could feel his touch as she lathered her body with soap.

The shower's steam filled the room leaving the mirror foggy. As Mona stepped out of the shower, she gently wiped the mirror with her hand, so she could see her face.

Her big brown eyes matched her light brown hair as she rang her long hair out with a towel. She brushed her hair as she stared into the mirror. She thought of how many weeks she had missed in school and tried to brush her thoughts away. She's been doing so well headed in the right direction for several years. But all her good efforts were slowly vanishing. Who was there to teach her to do better?

Who was there to teach her how to love? Her parents were long gone, and she's been on her own since childhood. The only person she looked up to was her sister. Mona helped run her sister's beauty supply store while attending community college on New York Blvd. For a while, everything was a breeze. Her grades were on point and she stayed away from unnecessary drama.

That was a great deal considering all the things she's endured over the years. After Mona's mother passed away, she and her sisters inherited a large life insurance policy. In which her older sister Kai invested her money and opened a beauty supply store where she and Mona ran the business together. Mona had very high hopes and planned to execute all her dreams and aspirations; but the ability for her to stay on the right track was an issue.

She tried her best to stay away from the fast life, but the streets kept calling her. The streets were all she knew. She had both book and street smarts and played both sides of the fence very well. Being in the drug game was just as addictive as the drug itself. Her mind was constantly battling with what's right and what's popping.

For the moment, Mona was chasing that money. She wanted to be fly as ever. Addicted to the cars, the clothes, the jewels, that fast pace was in her blood. Codes of the streets in cold weather. The epiphany of a black girl lost falling through the cracks. Blind sighted by the danger signs of drugs, passion, and murder. Due to the numbness of her soul, the streets didn't scare her one bit.

She embraced the streets with her whole heart and loved the leash that grabbed a hold of her. The phone in Mona's room rang as she curled her hair. The person on the other end, hung up before she could answer. *"Oh shit! That was Kema."* Mona thought. Staring at the phone on her bed. The temperature in the room was brisk and Mona could tell that it was cold outside as she dried her body with the towel.

She thought of the visit she had with Tony a couple of weeks ago, as she rubbed her legs with lotion. She couldn't believe that he was finally coming home, and she counted the days until she saw his face again. *"Tony was in prison for far too long."* Mona thought to herself. As she continued putting lotion on her arms and hands. Mona was prepared to pick Tony up in a weeks' time.

She made sure that specific date and time was clear, so she could be there when he got out of the pen. *"Oh, my goodness, look at the snow it looks beautiful."* Mona shouted. Excited about the snow as she opened the blinds in her bedroom. The sun was beaming but the ground was covered with white fluffy snow. Mona loved the winter time.

She loved to dress in ski jackets, tight jeans and timberlands with a fresh hat over top of her long hair. She walked into her closet to pick out a fresh outfit. She picked out some sky-blue denim jeans with a tight fitted sweater to match her royal blue ski jacket. Everything in Mona's apartment was brown, cream and beige. Her father's favorite colors. She kept such a tight bond with her mom and dad spiritually although they've been gone for several years.

It was 9AM as Mona glared at the clock while cooking herself some grits and eggs with a fresh cup of coffee. As she sat down to eat breakfast, her phone rang again. Mona looked at her phone as she sipped on her coffee. "Hello. Mona answered. "Hey what's up Sis? What's your plans for the day?

I need you to come through today to run the beauty supply store for me. I got something super important to do this morning." Kai mentioned. Smiling on the other side of the receiver. "Well, I was going to head over to the projects to see what the girls were up to. You know I forgot to pick up that money from Kema last night." Mona replied. Staring at her ass in the mirror. "I can get to the beauty supply store at about 10 AM, just let me make a couple rounds first."

Mona continued the conversation with her sister as she put on her timberlands. "Kai. Where the hell you gotta go? Must be somebody special because you don't leave your store for nobody." Mona laughed. As she teased her sister. "Listen Mona, just make sure to meet me soon as you finish okay."

Kai mentioned. Standing in the doorway of her beauty supply store on Merrick Blvd. Hanging up the phone, Mona grabbed her purse and her keys and headed out for the day. The snow looked beautiful because it hadn't been hit yet with all that slushy shit. On the way to Kema's crib, Mona drove through 40 projects, so she could get a bottle of Moet from the liquor store to take back over to her crib later that night.

Driving through the hood bumping MJB's my life; Mona made a left on Long Street and quickly parked down the hill in the Baisley projects. She listened to her song while singing her heart out along with Mary hitting every note. She just closed her eyes and felt every melody. As Mona sang, she was suddenly interrupted by a tap on the car window.

The loud tap on the window startled her a little as she looked over angrily to see who was fucking up her vibe. When Mona rolled down her window, she was ready to curse out the person who took her out of a moment of musical heaven. Her mood was switched instantly once she saw who was standing before her. Mona was totally shocked with her mouth wide open staring into Tony's smiling face.

Tony hollered. "What's up Mona? You still singing I see, open up this door and give your boy a hug." Tony opened the car door to receive a hug he'd been longing for-for ten years. "Damn man I missed the shit out of you Mona. Feels so good to be home." Tony squeezed Mona as tight as he could while he talked to her.

"Oh, my goodness Tony, let me look at you. What the fuck is going on? Why didn't you call me and tell me you were home? I thought you were coming home next week. I can't believe you are standing in front of me. I missed you so much." Mona started crying as she stared into Tony's eyes. She couldn't believe that he was standing right in front of her. "So many nights I cried myself to sleep wondering if you were safe from harm.

Thank you lord for bringing my best friend back to me." She just cried and hugged Tony as tight as she could. "Mona, my bad for not telling you I was coming a week earlier, I wanted to surprise you and the girls. Mona just stared at Tony with a smirk on her face. "Where is everybody? I came home last night.

My girl Lori came to pick me up from the pen." Tony explained himself as he opened Mona's car door to sit inside. "What's up with Kai and Niema? I haven't spoken to anyone since I got out. We gotta get The Clique together asap. There's a lot of bread in these streets and I want what's mines. Who's making moves in the projects? Put me on Mona. We have a whole lot of shit to catch up on and I got all day." Tony smiled. Looking at Mona who was still in shock.

Tony and Mona sat in her car discussing her moves and the moves of the hood. She also put him on to where his work and money was since he been in the pen. Mona saved half of Tony's bread and told him exactly where she stashed it. The Clique was back in full effect and Mona was the happiest chick on earth.

"Tony where do you want to go for lunch." Mona asked. Making a U-turn to park her car on the other side of the street. "We are going out to get something to eat soon as I get this paper from Kema. She should be at home right now. Mona's morning was set on going to Kema's crib to see if the girls bagged up the coke for tonight's shift and pick up the money she left the night before. "Ok cool we can go to Sammy's I'm fiending for some seafood.

Haven't eaten a good meal in years. Tony mumbled. While he rubbed his stomach. "Damn I haven't seen my girls in years. I want to see all their crazy asses." Today is a good day. Tony hollered. Stepping out of Mona's car. Walking up the hill, Tony was greeted by everybody in the hood. Nothing but smiling faces and sweet embraces approached his essence.

Tony!" Tony!" "Welcome home Bro." "When did you get back?" Sierra shouted. Wiping the white foam from around her ashy lips. Tony looked at Sierra and hollered. "What the fuck happened to you? I thought you stopped smoking that shit Si-Si damn. That shit just keep calling you huh!" Tony hugged Sierra with all his might. "You've gotta be stronger than that Sierra. Get your shit together!" Tony whispered.

As he slowly let go of Sierra's arm showing a real look of concern on his face. Si-Si just stared at him, licking the top of her gums with her tongue. "Tony I'm doing good I'm not on that shit no more." Sierra was lying through the little teeth she had left in her mouth. She didn't even believe herself.

It didn't take a rocket scientist to see that she just smoked some shit before she walked out of the building. Tony and Mona just stared at her. "Okay If you say so!" Tony mumbled. Walking passed Sierra, headed towards Kema's building. 'Knock… knock… knock. "Yo! Kema. Come open the door. Mona screamed. She shook the doorknob standing in front of her friend's apartment. Mona continued shaking the knob until Kema came to the door.

"Who the fuck is it?" Kema screamed. "Bitch it's me, open up the damn door." Mona replied. Still turning at the doorknob. Kema looked through the peephole and then yanked the door open holding onto her robe. Kema was butt ass naked with a black lace robe on. She looked like she had a hangover from drinking last night.

"Open up this door and let me in. What's going on up in here?" Tony asked. While rubbing his hands together. "Oh my god!" Tony! Oh, shit! When the fuck did you get out.?" Kema asked. Hugging Tony with her tits hanging out. Kema jumped up and down happy to see Tony standing in her apartment. Tony and Mona bussed out laughing watching Kema's tits bounce up and down as she screamed like a bat out of hell.

"Kema go put some damn clothes on girl, I'm not going anywhere." Tony chuckled. Kema ran to the back to get herself dressed. Kema's crib was nice and neat. She had a dark brown love seat and couch set with a big leopard carpet in the middle of the living room.

Kema loved the leopard print. That shit was spread all over her bed and in her bathroom as well. "Kema! What you got to eat up in here? You didn't learn how to cook yet? Gotta learn how to cook more than crack up in this mother fucker." Tony laughed. Joking around with his girls.

Kema came walking into the living room from the back fully dressed in her denim jeans and sneakers. "Shut up Tony you know damn well I know how to throw something together. I'm a grown ass woman now. I'm not no chef like Mona, but I get busy don't be trying to play me." Kema walked into the kitchen and opened the cabinet. She pulled out three stacks of cash and placed the money on the table. "Mona since Tony is back I might as well hand this money over to him."

"Oh Nah, do your thing." Tony interrupted. Signaling her to give the money to Mona. Tony knew his position, but he wanted to keep the ball rolling to see how they operated shit while he was away. "Listen we need to get all of the girls together and set up a meeting. I need to know everything that's been going on in the hood since I've been gone." As Tony sat down in the living room, Mona looked over at Kema and rolled her eyes while snatching the money off the table.

"Bitch don't be looking at me like that. I just needed to know who I was giving this money too." Kema snarled. Looking back at Mona with an attitude. "Shut the fuck up Kema. You know damn well you were supposed to give the money to me I don't give a fuck whose back, Tony know I be running shit around here." Tony looked at Mona and laughed.

"I see Ima have to put you on a leash. You a real firecracker! I like that." Tony mentioned. Staring at Mona with a smile. Mona smiled back as she got on her cell phone to call up Niema, Kizz & Kai to tell them the good news of Tony's return home. It was on and popping now that their main man was back on the scene. Mona told all the girls to meet her Tony and Kema at Sammy's in City Island.

Tony was dying to eat some seafood and couldn't wait to get to his favorite restaurant. All the time Tony served kept him humble within. He didn't interact with many people while he served his sentence. He did what he had to do, served his time and made it back home in one piece. Tony's girl Lori stayed connected to him the whole time.

She went on visits and gave him whatever he needed while he was locked away. "Now that you're back on the streets, you must be extra careful of who you fuck with while on parole." Mona mentioned. Counting the money that Kema gave her. "Listen I don't give a fuck about the police, parole or none of this shit. What they don't know, I'm sure not going to tell them.

Ima move like I been moving in these streets for years. If it wasn't for that bitch ass mother fucker Lem, I would've never gotten locked up in the first place. That nigga killed my man and he got dealt with. Now that I'm back, everything is going back to the way it was when I left." Tony didn't give a fuck about the law, because the law didn't give a fuck about him.

He knew exactly what he wanted, and he was eager to get everything back to the way it was before he went to prison. Tony was proud of Mona for holding on to his bread. He looked at her in a whole new light and respected her loyalty to him while he was away. Despite all the hardships she has been through in her life and all the shit she endured while he was in the pen; she never once betrayed him, and he loved the shit out her for that. Sitting up in Sammy's restaurant, Tony was feeling good as hell to be back with his family.

The aroma of lobsters, shrimps, and crab legs filled the air as the waitress brought over some fresh bread and water. "Are you ready to place your order?" The waitress asked, politely waiting for an answer.

As Tony looked up to reply to the waitress, Niema, Kizz and Kai came running towards the table screaming and hugging at Tony welcoming him home. "Tony! "My brother is home." Niema cried. Tony hugged his sister tight as she cried in his arms. Kai and Kizz soon followed hugging and kissing Tony over and over. Everyone was now back together again like old times. "Yeah! I want stuffed lobster with shrimps, king crab legs, a baked potato with chives and sour cream and a large strawberry daquiri."

The Clique smiled as Tony placed his order of food. Mona shouted. "I'll have what he's having." The waitress agreed as she took everyone's order at the table.

Kai and Kizz ordered king crab legs, with shrimp alfredo while Niema and Kema ordered some shrimps, oysters and clams, with a side of clam chowder. As everyone waited for their food Tony opened the conversation and asked who was running shit in the projects while he was away. "Whose hands is dirty in the hood Kai?"

Tony chuckled. While putting butter on his bread before he ate it. "Why are you asking me? I don't be in the hood like that. I be at my store running the beauty supply. I let Mona and Kema handle all of the dirty work." Kai answered. Laughing back at Tony. "Oh shit! No, you didn't just try to act like you don't got shit to do with our dealings like you don't be the main one sitting there when we all need to bag some shit up girl bye."

Mona hollered. Kai bussed out laughing as she sipped on her Hennessy. "Damn don't read me like that I was just playing. Can a sister get credit for running a legit business to back all this money we get from dealing these drugs on those streets? Give a bitch some credit where it's due." Kizz interrupted the conversation to speak to Tony.

"A couple of cats who use to re-up with Vince from South Road stepped in while you were gone and took over with the connect. They also let us do our thing on the strength of you and Vince. "You know Beno'? Dark skinned heavy-set guy with all the fronts in his mouth. Well, him and his brother Dirk' is running shit in the hood and they got a few trap houses set up near 40 projects as well." Kizz stirred at her Pina Colada when she finished talking.

"Oh, Beno stepped up huh! Tony blurted. While cracking into his crab leg. Beno been hustling since the beginning. He's been copping keys for a very long time and always did his own thing in the back streets on South Road. If this nigga stepped to you all when I got locked up, then he should have no problem falling back once I step to him." Tony mentioned.

Sipping on his strawberry daquiri. When Tony got locked up, Mona was sitting on a few kilos of coke that she had no idea how to get rid of on her own. She started hanging out at the after-hour spot and ran into Beno who was pushing kilos of coke and dope on a weekly basis.

Beno hollered at Mona one night and told her to hit him up, so she could sell him the keys of coke that Tony left behind to make some quick money. It was all she wrote after that. Once Beno bought the drugs, he asked The Clique if they could bag up for him and the ball just kept rolling. Beno didn't ask no questions.

He just wanted the work bagged up when he asked, paid for his services and let The Clique continue with whatever hustle they had beforehand. Nobody knew what was going down with Beno and The Clique because it was none of nobody's fucking business. Every time Beno came thru with a brick, The Clique would get paid and had his work bagged up waiting for him to make moves when he rolled out and the hustle stayed in heavy rotation.

Tony never had a problem with Beno because he never really saw him unless it was time to go re-up with the connect for some bricks on a humble. Tony was just impressed that The Clique managed to keep his shit a float without him all these years. "Ok Ima have to check him and his brother out asap." Tony mentioned. There was a clear understanding at the table as they all drank, ate good and celebrated.

"Speaking of Beno, there's his brother Dirk right there." Kizz blurted. Pointing in Dirk's direction. Tony looked over to see who Kizz was pointing to. He then saw Beno's brother waiting on line for a table. "Oh shit! He's going to live a long time. We were just talking about the mother fucker." "Listen, Ima check him out in a few, let me buss this food down and enjoy my first day back like an OG."

Tony and his girls enjoyed each other's company as they ate with Tony at Sammy's having a feast. The drinks were in rotation and Tony was feeling good as hell. You could see the excitement all over his face. "I really love the shit out of all of you. Thank you for remaining loyal and not letting anyone in on your business. Let's keep these nosey mother fuckers guessing. From this point on.

I'm stepping back in with the connect and running shit in my hood. I got a few cats up in Harlem who use to move bricks with Sammy and Vince that's ready to plug me in on a much bigger connect. You all don't have to worry about shit, just keep doing what you been doing, and everything will be gravy." Tony continued. "Kai, you stay at the beauty supply store and hold shit down on the business tip.

I'm going to chat with my man Clay' who has a couple warehouses up in Harlem. He got a nice joint that I can rent out on a humble. As Tony put the girls on to all the moves he was making, Mona got up to use the restroom and Kai followed right behind her. "Look who I saw today dipping through the projects. Kai whispered. Standing on the line to use the rest room, grinning at her sister showing her friend's number on her cell phone.

Kai had a crush on Peter since elementary school. Although they went their separate ways, made kids of their own and led total different lives. They always managed to find their way back to each other hugged up in the bed like love birds in lust. "Well look who flew over the coocoo nest.

Where the hell he been at wit his lying ass." Mona smirked and giggled staring at the number. Mona continued. "You two just can't stay away from each other damn." Mona snarled. "He just got out of the joint too. He came home last week. I just saw him before I came here. Ooh honey, he looks good as hell too. Ima hit that up with the quickness before he gets a whiff of all these thirsty ass hoes.

You know how that fresh dick get home; everybody and they mama wants to suck it." Mona bussed out laughing. "Hell yeah, the whole hood be fucking the same dude at once fighting over one dick." Kai agreed with Mona shaking her head. The line at the rest room started going down as Mona and Kai entered.

Walking into the rest room, both girls noticed Tony's girlfriend Lori coming out of one of the bathroom stalls. "Hold up! "Isn't that Lori right there?" Kai whispered. As she turned to look the other way, so Lori wouldn't recognize her. "Hell yeah, that's her. What the fuck is she doing in here." Mona replied. Her eyes were wide open almost popping out of her head. Lori stood there fixing her hair and began washing her hands before she exited the rest room.

Kai and Mona went and used the stalls on the other side of the rest room, so Lori wouldn't bump into them once she finished. Lori then exited the rest room and went back into the seating area on the other side of the restaurant. "Oh my, I wonder who she's here with. Does Tony know that she's here? Let me find out that bitch is creeping like a side hoe."

Mona went in on Lori thinking the worst because she knew in her gut that-- that bitch was up to no good. Kai continued to shake her head as she washed her hands. "Well we about to find out right mother fucking now. Kai replied. Drying her hands under the dryer. Both Mona and Kai exited the bathroom and went to the other side of the restaurant to see where Lori had gone. They didn't go all the way to the other side, because they didn't want to risk the chance of Lori seeing them at all.

"Fuck it, let's go back to our table and put Tony on to his little precious fucking Lori." Mona whispered. Rolling her eyes. Mona never had anything against Lori she just didn't fuck with any chicks that Tony fucked with. She loved Tony very much and didn't want to get in the middle of his affairs.

Mona and Kai returned to their table. They didn't want to bring down the mood, but they just had to tell Tony who they just saw. Tony was sitting at the table cracking jokes with the girls having a good ole time. It took you long enough; I thought you two went home. Tony chuckled. Looking at Mona cheesing. "Funny Tony I'm never leaving your sight ever again." Mona replied. Smiling back at him.

Niema bussed out laughing because she knew that Mona was dead ass serious by the sound of her voice. "Listen Tony, on some real shit, I don't know how to tell you this but me and Kai just saw your girl Lori in the rest room. Mona blurted out quickly while popping shrimps into her mouth. Kai just sipped on her drink nodding her head up and down agreeing with what Mona just said. Niema shouted.

"What the fuck is she doing in Sammy's? Who would she be up in here with? You with us!" Tony was looking at Mona like she was crazy. "You didn't know she was in here Tony?" Mona asked. Waiting anxiously for an answer. "Nah! I didn't even know I was coming here this shit is news to me. I just got the fuck home last night. We all about to find out right now who she here with and it better not be with a nigga.

Tony guzzled his drink before he got up to see what the fuck Mona and Kai was talking about. As Tony got up from the table all the girls got up with him following suit. Niema told the waitress that they weren't done with their table they were just going to the rest room. The waitress just stared at Niema as she ran away from her to catch up with her clique. Tony began looking around to see if he saw Lori.

He hadn't seen her yet. Tony hollered. You sure it was her Mona, you may need glasses because I don't see her in here. Low and behold, soon as he blurted out those words; there Lori was sitting in a booth on the other side of the restaurant with Beno's brother Dirk. "Oh, shit Tony, there she goes right there. Kai screamed. Pointing at the table. Tony and the girls couldn't believe their eyes. Lori was sitting with Dirk eating dinner, laughing and flirting. Dirk was feeding her shrimps and grabbing a hold of her hands.

"Oh, this bitch got me fucked up." Tony mumbled. Walking over to the table. "I see this is how you was doing me while I was locked up. You a dirty fucking bitch, come here. Tony rushed the table and threw all the food and drinks onto Lori and the floor. "Yo! What the fuck."

Dirk snarled. Shocked at Tony's rage. Lori just sat there looking stupid with shrimps and lobster sauce all over her sweater. "This is how you do me bitch. You didn't think I'd be up in here huh! Well, you are sadly mistaken hoe." Tony grabbed Dirk out of his seat and yanked him up against the wall. "You knew Lori was my girl mother fucker. You knew that shit! The whole hood knew.

"How long you been fucking with her? The whole time I been in the pen." Tony banged Dirk's head against the wall before he walked over to Lori taking his rings off her fingers. "Bitch you sitting up in here with the next nigga with my mother fucking jewels on that I brought you.

You better be lucky I just got out of the joint I would beat the shit out of your ass right in this restaurant." Dirk walked back towards the table shouting. "This shit ain't even necessary. You are making a big scene in here over some pussy." When Dirk turned around, Tony shouted. "No, you the mother fucking pussy, punching Dirk in the face knocking him out cold right up in Sammy's restaurant.

The Clique was in shock staring at Dirk sleeping on the floor like he was at home in his bed. "You should have never crossed me bitch." Tony was fuming! He couldn't believe that his girl was fucking around on him and lying to him about everything. Every letter, every conversation, every moment he shared with her, was all a lie.

All the sweet memories of the girl who took him to cloud nine was destroyed in one split second. "Mona whip this bitch ass. Tony shouted. He then walked up to the table yanking the chain he brought Lori off her neck. Mona walked up to Lori and punched her right in her face.

Lori sat at the table crying as Tony left her there to sit with her date who was knocked out on the floor. Mona ran to the table they were sitting at and left the waitress a huge tip after paying for the bill. They all ran out of the restaurant and disappeared before the police were called. "That bitch got a lot of fucking nerve doing what she did. I can't believe she was just in there with Beno's brother." Mona shouted. Opening her car door. "Oh, my goodness Tony you just knocked Dirk out."

Oh my god! This shit is far from fucking over." Kema squealed. Tony looked at Kema with no fucks to give. "Kema shut the fuck up! Why you so concerned about Dirk? You fucking that nigga or something? Fuck him and fuck that bitch Lori too." Everybody stared at Kema for a minute as she stood in silence. Mona and the girls didn't know what to say. No matter what happened, they had Tony's back one hundred percent.

The Clique couldn't believe what just went down. After everyone hopped into their rides, Tony told Mona to take him to Lori's crib over by Springfield high school. On the way to Lori's house, Tony dozed off as he pictured the girl that he loved in the arms of another man.

He saw visions of Lori fucking and sucking Dirk in his head while he was away thinking she was loyal to him. Tony sat in the passenger seat disappointed and hurt. Everyone pulled up to Lori's place. The Clique and Tony jumped out of their rides and went up in Lori's crib. They gathered all of Tony's belongings. His clothes, jewels, shoes, sneakers, placed them into large garbage bags, then piled everything into Mona's trunk.

Tony wanted to take everything back that he brought Lori, but he left it, so she can see that there would never be another nigga like him. He then went to Lori's room where he left his safe, opened it up, took all his money out then placed it into one of his duffle bags.

After getting everything out of Lori's crib, he told Mona to take him to her place. "Listen Mona I run these fucking streets. Dirk should've never touched my fucking girl. If Beno got a problem with me, we'll settle this shit once I see him. Right now, I'm going to your crib to take a shower and get some rest. Tony reclined the seat back and closed his eyes. Mona just looked at him and slightly rolled her eyes.

"Well fine with me shit, I was going to take you to my crib anyway. You don't have to ask me twice." Mona giggled. Turning the music up in her ride. She said she wasn't letting Tony out of her sight. I guess you get what you ask for. Tony is now a free man from the system and free from his relationship.

In this game called life, you never know the cards you're dealt you just gotta count your blessings and play your hand right. Just like a game of spades, never ever renege on yourself. The Clique laughed about everything that just happened. "What a way to celebrate your first day home. It's going to be a cold ass winter." Mona smiled. Waving at her clique while pulling off with her best friend by her side.

CHAPTER 2

TONY

"It was extremely cold outside. The temperature had to be about 12 degrees, but it felt like below zero. The heat was on full blast and Tony was snuggled up under the covers laying in Mona's bed. When he woke up, he looked around for Mona and saw that she wasn't on the other side of the bed. Mona was already up making breakfast listening to her song creep by TLC in the kitchen. Pancakes and eggs with maple bacon filled the air as Tony walked into the kitchen. "I go to reach for a morning hug and you already up doing your thing.

I'm not mad at you at all, because them pancakes smell good like a mother fucker right now." Tony walked up to Mona and gave her a kiss on the cheek. Mona smiled. As she battered the pancake mix and poured it into the frying pan. "I thought you would like a nice home cooked breakfast this morning being that it's your first week home with the family. You haven't seen shit yet Tony, wait until you taste my recipes I gets busy in the kitchen."

Mona giggled. Shaking her ass while she placed some cheese into the scrambled eggs. "Ima catch the itis up in this joint. Cooking like that I won't never leave, keep it up. Tony mentioned. Watching Mona cook breakfast made Tony feel warm inside. He hadn't felt this way in a long time and was happy to be in the presence of his home girl again.

"Yesterday was the bomb Mona. That food was slamming at Sammy's. I haven't had king crab legs in ten mother fucking years. That shit was good as hell. I could have smacked everybody mama in that joint. I Really enjoyed our lunch date Mona word." Tony thanked Mona for bringing him to his favorite restaurant with the girls. Being back at home was a breath of fresh air for Tony.

It got real lonely and dark for a few years upstate in the pen. Tony wanted it that way. He didn't want to be a burden to anyone while he was in prison. His time in the pen was his alone to take like a man and he did just that. You come to find that in life some of the toughest battles are given to the strongest soldiers.

What doesn't kill you only makes you stronger. Tony walked out of the kitchen into the living room thinking about his pops as he reminisced about his past lives. Ever since Tony was a youngster, he's managed to make shit happen through the guidance of his uncle Vince. Vince took Tony under his wing after his father was murdered in the projects when he was five years old.

Tony's father was a major connect to pure cocaine up in Harlem. His father Romeo was a real street hustler who knew and sold bricks to every drug dealer who was getting it. Romeo's life ended tragically one day when he was held at gun point and robbed of ten kilos of cocaine by two dirty cops who took his life and ran off with his drugs.

Tony's father was shot 6 times in the chest and left for dead on the roof of one of the buildings in the projects. Romeo was very close to Vince and Sammy and they made a whole lot of money together until he got murdered. After his murder, Vince went on a killing spree and robbed every connect he thought had something to do with the dirty cops who killed his friend. He set an example in the hood just in case a mother fucker thought shit was sweet.

As for Tony, he got turned on to the drug game at the tender age of ten. Vince put him on to the game before he became a teenager where he began pistol whipping cats, fucking with grown women, driving cars, he was doing everything under the sun. He had more chicks than the goons in the crew who looked out for him.

Tony grew up in the fast lane and there wasn't a damn thing anybody could do about it. He belonged to the streets and in the streets, he was highly respected. He never really had a childhood. While his friends played kickball, sports, and tag, he was doing grown men shit pushing bricks through all boroughs with Vince, meeting connects and putting a stamp in them streets early. He was a drug dealer before he learned how to pedal a bike.

Life as a kid pretty much didn't happen for Tony. He grew up living the fast life and saw a lot of shit that the average adult couldn't bear. The streets were in his heart and soul. His loyalty and love for Vince was unconditional and could never be broken and that's what made him special. Trafficking drugs was all he knew.

His family never worried about him because he was protected by the most ruthless drug lords in Queens. Tony was the rich kid that loved to splurge with his friends and family. He was never the type of person to let people do shit for him. If he had it, you had it with no hesitation; especially if you were cool people. If he didn't have it, he'd stick something up to get it.

Tony did everything he had to do to make ends meet. Especially when his back was against the wall; it was a wrap for anyone who got in his way. Don't fuck around and be around Tony or his goons when shit hit the fan. Fuck around and be a dead man. Stuck out of luck with no bucks. That street life was rough, and Tony was tough and took no shorts from nobody when it came to getting that paper.

When Tony got out of jail, his cousin set him up with a construction job to keep the police off his back whenever he paid a trip up to the parole office. He worked four days a week from 8am to 3pm and made the required number of hours to keep him a float.

The construction site he worked on had a lot of coke heads and users on the job and that made it easy to come back and forth to work selling large quantities of coke to co-worker's, friends and even bosses of the site all wanted to score. Cocaine is a functional drug where a user could hit a bump of coke and go on with their daily schedule.

Tony kept all his dealings and business on the low and made sure everyone who he fucked with at work; knew someone he knew to keep from getting set up on the job.

Plenty apartments were on lock in the projects and Tony's aunt's crib was one of them. These apartments and trap houses kept the drug dealers in business. A place to stash and bag up drugs was the main part of the hustle. Everyone was on the same page and looked out for one another no matter what. After Tony got arrested, shit started getting crazy. People in the hood started losing their lives for their territory and the new coke boys started moving in from different neighborhoods.

It was the same game with different people. It hurt Tony to the core to take that bid and lose so many years of his life, but Tony took his bid hard body and dealt with the struggle of prison life the best way he knew how which was calm, cool, collective and on his own.

Spending ten years in jail has taught Tony a lot mentally. He never let the walls of prison break his spirit. Life has its ups and downs and bumpy roads and sometimes you've gotta learn from the bad times to get to the good. Life is a rollercoaster of experiences and lessons. Most people learn from their mistakes and some people are very hard to teach. Mona walked towards the living room where Tony stood looking out of the window at the snow.

"I'm glad you enjoyed yourself Tony, I enjoyed myself too until the drama started." Mona giggled. Covering her face as she thought about the incident with Lori. "Word! Everything was great until this bitch Lori brought that whack ass dude to the restaurant to get punched in his grill."

Tony looked at Mona laughing as he thought about Dirk knocked out in Sammy's restaurant. "Oh, my goodness Tony. You are off the hook." Mona shouted. Looking at him with a glare. "What am I supposed to tell Beno when he asks me about his brother? Oh, my god!" "I can't believe that shit just happened." Mona continued talking as she poured herself a glass of wine.

"We supposed to be celebrating you coming home and people getting knocked the fuck out, that shit was hilarious." Mona could not stop staring at Tony. "Man, fuck Beno! Yo! What the fuck is a Beno anyway? Tony shouted. Staring at Mona sitting on the sofa. "What the hell you expect me to do? It wasn't my fault. The bitch was sitting up in Sammy's like she didn't even have a relationship.

Like she didn't just pick me up from the pen the night before. That bitch could have gotten killed yesterday she got off easy. I better not see that chick Lori I might choke the shit out of her if I do." Tony got up and looked out of the window thinking of how foul his ex-girl did him. "You don't need to do anything else Tony.

Listen, let Lori be, you have done enough. You just got back from prison and she is not worth it at all. I know she is feeling fucked up because she got caught red handed and it ain't no coming back from that. Believe me she is probably crying her heart out over you right now thinking of ways to get your ass back. Lori is a sneaky conniving bitch. I never liked her from the jump.

Just wash your hands with that chick Tony you don't need to be getting locked up for kicking her ass. Please leave her alone. If she calls the cops on you, I swear I'm going to kill that bitch myself." Mona pleaded with Tony gulping down the rest of her wine. "I'm going to give Beno a call tomorrow and let him know what happened. I don't feel like dealing with this shit today. Dirk should have never taken Lori on a date. What was he thinking? Lord knows how long they've been seeing each other.

She probably been fucking him all these years lying through her teeth acting like she's all loyal and shit. She really played herself Tony. I can't believe she tried to play you soon as you came home that bitch is bold."

"Yeah, I can't believe it either." Tony replied. Counting all the money that he took out of the safe at Lori's house. Tony counted $50,000 with Mona in her living room. The Money he left at Lori's crib, was moneys he made moving bricks with his man Sammy out in Harlem before he got killed. Lori never thought to open the safe because she kept a bigger stash that Tony left in her safety deposit box when he got locked up.

"I'm disappointed and happy at the same damn time. At least I know what type of chick I'm dealing with. If I would have found her with this dude at her crib; I think I would have killed them both. I think it's best I found out the way that I did, because the way I'm thinking right now, is not a good look at all. I'm not worried about Beno, he a little pussy.

Ima definitely speak to him too when you call him."

Mona just sat in the chair listening to her partner in crime.

"What I do believe in, is me and you." Tony whispered into

Mona's ear as he passed by walking towards the kitchen.

"What's going on with your writing Mona? You still writing

them stories. You had me open in the pen with your short

stories I love that shit, those joints are popping. Keep that

shit up, I'll support you all the way to the top."

Mona couldn't stop smiling as she listened to Tony talk

about her stories. "Yeah! I still have my stories Tony. I

haven't been writing that much lately, been too busy chasing

this paper." Ever since Tony got locked up, Mona vowed to

get her life together and stay on a straight arrow.

She got a few 9-5 jobs here and there put herself in school and kept up with her self-support groups for two years. As time went on, she started missing all the real paper she used to make bagging up dope and coke and went back to the fast lane. The drug game is nothing at all to play with. Once you get a costumed to living in the fast lane, it gets very hard getting out. Especially when you're running with the same people you ran with before you left.

The streets had a funny way of sucking you right back into its web. Dealing drugs was a piece of cake for Mona. She had everything taken care of being that her sister had a legit business. She knew she could count on her sister to clean her money by working alongside of her as an investor if anything ever popped off.

Mona took off her timberlands and pants and walked around in her tank top and boy shorts. "Well whatever you do, don't give that up baby. Creative people are unique and rare. When you got a special gift you gotta use it to the best of your ability. God bless the child that's got his/her own. Believe me, you got it Mona."

Tony always supported Mona since they were kids vice/versa. He admired her strength and potential. Mona went to her bedroom to get a stack of manuscripts that she had written through the years since Tony's been incarcerated. She called Tony, so he could look through them with her. "Thanks Tony! I appreciate you for always believing in me. Mona placed the manuscripts on the dresser.

I can't thank you enough Tony. You are the only person who truly believed in me." Mona continued to thanked Tony while kissing him on his cheek. When Mona turned to walk away. Tony grabbed her and kissed her on her lips. Tony rubbed his fingers through Mona's hair and tongued her down.

He started kissing her lips, her face, down to her neck, then he lifted her shirt and kissed her breasts. Mona was hot and wet giving herself to Tony. She moaned as he continued sucking her breasts. Tony briefly stopped grabbing Mona by the hand leading her to the bed. Mona was swept away ready to make love to the love of her life. She couldn't be happier. Mona relaxed on the bed while Tony kissed her belly button. Moving his tongue down to her cherry.

Mona moaned uncontrollably as Tony sucked the life out of her kitty. He licked and teased and kissed her kitten until she couldn't take it anymore. Then he turned her around and fucked the shit out of her. Tony hadn't had any pussy in ten years. Mona felt every stroke as he smacked her on her ass. UHH! … "Tony! I love you Tony, fuck me."

Mona loved every inch of his huge manhood. Mona's phone rang, but she ignored it as Tony continued making love to her pulling her hair while he kissed her. "You feel so fucking good, I love this pussy." Tony whispered into Mona's ear as he long stroked her nice and slow. Tony was completely satisfied with what just happened. He loved Mona all his life. He just never wanted to ruin their friendship.

Lying next to Mona felt so right. She completed him. Mona was the female version of Tony and he loved everything about her. Tony and Mona just stayed in the bed hugged up stuck together like glue. Mona smiled at Tony as she got up to use the rest room. When Mona went into the bathroom, Tony just rested in the bed collecting his thoughts.

He always knew he would wind up fucking with Mona, he just didn't know when that day would arrive. Tony couldn't get Lori out of his head at the same time. Mona's phone rang again, vibrating on her night stand. Tony got up to look at who was calling her. Picking up the phone, he saw that it was Beno on the other end. "Hello!" Tony answered. "Can I speak to Mona? Who's this?" Beno asked. "This is Tony! Is this Beno?" Tony asked. "Yeah Tony this is Beno.

I heard about what happen at the restaurant. That shit was fucked up how you did my brother. If I were in your shoes I would have done the same shit." Tony looked at the phone with a confused look on his face. "I told Dirk not to fuck with Lori, but he did it anyway. Dirk had to know you were home I know Lori isn't that stupid to keep that shit a secret. Dirk is not feeling this situation at all Tony.

I just thought I'd call to relay the message to Mona. He's tight that you knocked him out over this shit and he may want to retaliate. I am doing business with Mona and she has a few kilos of coke at Kema's crib. Now I am calling you, so we can come to some sort of understanding and handle this shit like men. My brother on the other hand, I don't know if he feels the same way at this present time.

I will be meeting up at Kema's crib this evening. We could either meet up in the projects or we can pick another location to talk further and settle our differences. Beno just came at Tony like a man. He didn't want any beef with Tony but at the same time Dirk was Beno's brother and Tony didn't trust a word he was saying. "Listen man, I just came home I wasn't looking to get into any problems.

Dirk fucked my girl and he got dealt with end of story. Mona and The Clique are my girl's and whatever business you did with them while I was in the pen is finished. Once you get the kilos you left at Kema's, their business with you is over. All the connects you got I got so there is no need for my girls to do business with you any further unless you want to cut me in on a piece of the pie."

You a good dude Beno and I respect your hustle. You've been down for a long time since the beginning. Whatever we need to discuss has already been said. If we see each other in the hood so be it. My girls & I appreciate the services that were available while I was away. If you need to hit me or Mona up for any reason, feel free to call me or come through." Tony let Beno know that his services were no longer needed.

Beno agreed to Tony's wishes and both Tony and Beno ended their conversation. When Mona came out of the bathroom she sat in the chair in the bedroom and listened to everything that Tony said. "Yo! Mona, come in here." Tony screamed. Not knowing she was already sitting in the room.

"So, I take it you heard everything I said huh. Mona didn't say a word. She just stared at Tony from across the room. Tony didn't like the silence one bit as he walked over to Mona and grabbed her by the shoulders. "You ever fucked Beno? Answer me!" Tony looked into Mona's big brown eyes and kissed her on the lips. Mona kissed Tony back as he rubbed his fingers through her hair.

"Yes, Tony I fucked him once five years ago. You can ask him yourself. It only happened once and it only last two minutes. I fucked with him one night on a humble. We were getting fucked up sniffing coke and drinking all night his dick didn't even work it was so fucking little he just ate my kitten and gave me some cash to go shopping the next day.

Don't be mad at me Tony, we weren't even together. At least I tell you the truth and I'm not sneaky like that lying ass bitch Lori. Tony threw Mona on the bed and explained to her how much he loves her. "I love you Mona. I know we weren't together baby. I don't know how this shit is going to work between you and me.

We are too dangerous for each other. I can't resist fucking you. I loved you since the first day we met. I'm telling you right now if I find out you are fucking anybody Ima fuck you up. Don't fucking play with me. Tony whispered. Kissing Mona on the lips. "Whatever you did while I was locked up, scratch that shit. From this point on, we in this shit together. You're my Bonnie and I'm your Clyde. We're In this shit together forever."

Mona just stared at Tony crying while he talked to her agreeing with every word. At this point Tony didn't give a fuck about Dirk, Lori or Beno. All he cared about was sitting right in front of his face the whole time. Tony been through so many different dilemma's in his lifetime with friendships, family, relationships, the law and through all these situations, he could always count on Mona.

Tony put all his eggs into Lori when Mona is the one who had his heart. Tony was so frustrated and angry thinking of how many years he lost fucking with that snake ass bitch. "Come on Mona let's get dressed, take a ride with me uptown." Tony had an inside connect who was related to a dear friend of his, that he planned to meet up with to get the ball rolling again in his favor.

Vince's partner Sammy that got killed, introduced Tony to his nephew Clay' a couple of months before he was murdered. Before Tony came home, Vince reminded Mona to have Tony check out the connect soon as he touched N.Y. Clay was a hustler who pushed bricks from Harlem to South Side Jamaica Queens. Clay moved through Queens daily, but he lived in Spanish Harlem.

His connects were inherited by Vince and his uncle Sammy. When Sammy got murdered, all his drugs, guns, money and connects were stashed at his nephew's warehouse who also lived a few blocks away from him.

After Clay buried his uncle, he partnered up with his brother and contacted the Italian connect that Vince and Sammy rolled with out in Long Island and kept shit moving ever since. Clay stayed fresh. He was a fly mother fucker.

Tall and brown skinned, but very low key and he gave you the shirt off his back if he really fucked with you. He reached out to Tony while he was locked up and put him on to the shit he was doing in the streets while he was away. He told Tony that he would have a lot of things set up for him once he made it back home. Tony wanted to make good with Clay's offer and planned on meeting up with him asap.

Tony and Mona cleaned up, showered and got dressed for the evening. Mona washed the dishes from breakfast, then took some catfish out of the freezer to thaw so she could fry it when she returned to the crib later that night. "Ooh! It's cold as fuck out here. Tony snarled. Throwing his hoody on his head. "You should have put on your jacket Tony. Mona replied. Would you like me to go and get it for you?

We right in front of the crib. Mona stood in front of her building playing in the snow waiting for Tony to answer her. "Yeah go get it for me Mona. Get the beige ski jacket and my hat. Tony answered. Staring at Mona's ass. Mona went back upstairs to get the jacket. She smiled as she waited for the elevator. She hadn't smiled in a long time. She had an empty void within her for many years.

The thought of her and Tony together blew her mind. It was one of her wildest dreams coming true. She didn't want to risk their relationship either, she just wanted them both to satisfy each other in every way possible. Mona didn't know how she was going to tell the girls about her and Tony fucking with each other. She just laughed at the thought of what they would say when they found out.

Mona went into the crib and grabbed Tony's jacket and hat from out of the closet. When Mona came back outside, she saw Tony talking to someone on the phone and he looked like he didn't like the conversation. "Tony what's wrong? What is it now?" Mona asked. Closing the car door. Tony was still on the phone shaking his head from side to side.

"Ok calm down Niema, we will be right there give us a few minutes. We coming to you right now." Tony waved his hand at Mona signaling her that he would be right with her in a second. When he hung up the phone, he looked at Mona with a disgusted look on his face. "What happened Tony? Tell me. Is everything okay?" Mona asked. Anxiously. "Sierra is fucking dead!

She just overdosed and died right in the lobby of Kema's building." Mona just stood there shocked for a half a minute. "Get the fuck out of here Tony. You playing with me, right? Sierra is dead! Oh, my goodness. She just couldn't walk away from the drugs it kept calling her. "Oh, my god Si-Si. I'm so sorry this happened to you." Mona cried as Tony drove to the projects.

Tony pulled up at the light on Baisley & New York Blvd. There were mad dudes crossed the street at Popeyes drinking and smoking banging music in their rides. Few cats hollered at Tony as he passed through. Tony beeped the horn and kept riding towards Baisley Projects. "Damn I just can't relax for nothing what the fuck. Every time I turn around its some bullshit. I told Sierra to leave that shit alone damn."

Tony was frustrated that he had to go to the projects to see his childhood friend dead. "Yeah! "This shit is crazy. That is the hand that was dealt her way. Everyone has their demons Tony, whether it's drinking, weed, cocaine, crack, heroin, pill popping, sex, the addiction just calls you and sucks you in deeper into its whole.

If you are not strong enough to maintain yourself, you can lose all self-awareness, control, health, wealth and stability. No one on earth is ever perfect. We all make choices and with these choices carry a continuation of consequences. What you do with the choices you make is always up to you." Mona continued. "Tony this is something that was destined to happen. We all told Sierra more than a dozen times, shit we even tell ourselves not to fuck with the drugs we bag up. That's the oldest rule in the book.

Never get high on your own supply." Mona stated. Tony reached the corner of Foch and New York Blvd. "Listen, you can't force a mother fucker not to use drugs. That's something that a person can only do on their own. It's an action that must be made from deep within.

Tony replied. Parking the car down the hill. "Sierra was sick! Mona shouted. "She had a disease. She was addicted to a substance that took control of her soul. She was doing so well for a couple of years too. Damn! She was working again, she got her own place headed in the right direction. Sierra was also an attractive young woman at one point in her life. Her downfall was that nigga she loved and trusted so much who beat her down both mentally and physically. They used to smoke crack together like it was a competition." Mona continued.

"Her poor body had gotten so slim and she probably was unable to take the abuse any longer." Tony just looked over at Mona with emotion in his eyes. "One of life's biggest tragedies is losing the ability to think.

The mind is very powerful. What you feed it molds you like a plant to a seed. Remember the shit that I say to you Mona. Never forget it." Pulling up in the projects, there were cops all over the place. Tony pulled out immediately from down the hill and parked the car in the back streets then him and Mona walked up the block. Walking up the hill, everyone was outside. The ambulance had arrived, but Sierra's body was still lying on the floor in the lobby.

Niema, Kema and Kizz were standing outside of the building crying. Sierra's Mom just hugged her daughter who was no longer, blue in the face with foam all around her mouth lying there lifeless. "Damn, this shit is fucked up." Tony mumbled. He then walked over to his sister and gave her a hug.

The Clique hugged each other and cried as Sierra lay waiting for the coroner to come and take her to the morgue. The energy in the hood was fucked up. The wind was blowing, and the snow covered the ground cold as fuck. "We gotta give Sierra a proper funeral. We must help Sierra's family send her away in style." Kizz cried. She was hysterical, staring at her friend's dead body. "Yeah! "We will be there for her and make sure her family has everything they need."

Tony replied. He shed real tears in front of his girls. Tony was feeling some type of way. No matter what happened, Si-Si was a part of the family. She was a part of The Clique. Every memory that the girls shared growing up Sierra was there. Her death hit home, and it showed us it was coming for her way before her life ended.

Sierra was crying for help in a big way. But nobody could rescue her. There's just something about death that grabs the emotions of the soul. No matter how hard you are or how tough, when someone passes away that you care for, you become a victim of their circumstance. Death is always a hard pill to swallow. No matter what the situation is. All the memories all the love all the tender moments just hit you all at once like a brick.

Tony hadn't been home for two whole days yet and he already witnessed an enormous amount of pain and frustration. This is the life we lived in the hood. We took the good with the bad and faced it with every ounce of strength we had. "Hey sis me and Mona got some shit to take care of we will come through to your crib when we finish.

Come on Mona." Tony hugged his sister and the girls then grabbed Mona by her hand and walked back down the hill. Niema and Kizz stared at Mona and Tony holding hands and they just laughed. Love you Tony and Mona don't forget to come to my house soon as you get back; I'm cooking tonight. Niema shouted. Sitting on the bench with Kema and Kizz. Watching Sierra's body lay in the lobby like that was crazy.

The police were out investigating the scene being annoying. Nobody in the hood said a mother fucking thing to the police. Everyone just wanted the police to hurry the fuck up and get Sierra to the morgue instead of fishing around the hood for answers they never were going to get. The streets are always talking, but never to the police.

Only a snitch ass nigga will do shit like that. The dynamics of the game is to make money. These crackers make money in these hospitals and pharmacies every fucking day the legal way. The system is designed to beat the black man down while they do the same shit they lock us up for. All this drug shit was designed to destroy the black community. It was man made and these projects were invented by the same devils who enslaved us over 600 years ago.

"Listen nobody putting a fucking gun to your head telling you to smoke crack. Every human being is responsible for their own actions. You can't blame a soul for the decisions you make in life. "Yeah, I have my demons, we all do. I bag up drugs in the hood, but if I don't do it, somebody else will I tell you that much.

A mother fucker is going to smoke that shit regardless. It doesn't make me right, but it doesn't make me wrong either. We grew up doing this shit. This world is full of crazy shit. You gotta get to that bag by any means. Survival of the fittest only the strong survive. & That's with any given situation." Niema preached some real hood shit sitting on the bench smoking a blunt with her friends.

Leaving the projects with Mona, Tony ran into one of his good friends from way back. They talked and kicked it for a minute about the police and how Sierra's body still didn't get picked up yet. "This shit is crazy how a mother fucker in the hood gotta wait for hours to get some help or some service when shit like this happens.

Let some shit like this happen where the crackers live. What? Them crackers would be picked up and dusted off and carried to the hospital asap. White people. Them some simple mother fuckers. It's amazing how much of an effect you can have on people. That is the one thing that seizes to amaze me." Tony's friend sat down the hill with him and kicked it for a hot hour. Mona sat on the bench talking to one of her little cousins reminiscing on the good ole days.

Mona went to the liquor store to pick up some liquor from around the corner. Her and Tony decided to stay in the hood and ride this shit out until the coroner came to pick up their friend. Tony didn't feel like taking that ride uptown feeling the way he was feeling. His concentration level wasn't on deck at all.

He was happy to be home but since he's been home there's been nothing but drama. Tony's just wanted to relax and get his mind right. "Here Tony. Are you ok? I just brought us some hypnotic and Hennessy." Mona sat next to Tony on the bench with the drinks and cups in her hands. "Oh, Cool I can use a drink right now word. Come on Mona lets go back up the hill with the girls." Tony grabbed the Henny and headed back up the hill with Mona.

"You sure you want to go back up there and see Si-Si like that. We can still get out of here if you want. Mona mentioned. Following Tony up the hill. "Nah! We gotta stay here with The Clique and face this shit together. No matter what Sierra was going through or how she lived her life she still was our friend and we need to be there for her.

Tony reached the top of the hill and handed the drinks to Niema. The Clique just sat on the bench together and drank pouring, out liquor for their childhood friend. "Ain't this a about a bitch." Niema snarled. Pouring a shot of Hennessy into a cup. Niema took a shot straight to the head staring at Sierra in the building on the floor.

"When the fuck are these mother fuckers coming to get her? Why does this process take so long? This shit doesn't make a bit of sense. Kizz was pissed and wanted answers as to why does a person have to be subjected to walking out of their home to see a dead body lying on the floor like it's a piece of garbage. "Kizz this shit right here will never make sense. The only thing we can do at this point is be strong for one another and hold each other down.

I promise we are all going to be straight mark my words." As soon as Tony marked his words, Beno came walking up the hill. "What the fuck does this nigga want. I swear to god I don't got time for the fucking dramatics I'm bound to kill a mother fucker right now. Mona I'm telling you right now, this nigga makes one wrong move and he's dead.

Mona and the girls just stared at Beno as he walked up the hill through the projects. "Tony don't say anything, just hear him out and see what he has to say. I'm sure he is not going to start no shit while these police and ambulance are out here. He's not that stupid. There is a time and a place for everything and right now is just not the time. Hey Beno." Mona shouted. Giving him a pound on the hand.

"What's up Mona. What the fuck happened over here?" Beno asked. Staring at the body that was laying on the floor in the lobby. Mona just stared at Sierra for a minute without saying a word. "Beno, that's Sierra under that sheet. She overdosed this afternoon and fell out right there in the lobby." Beno just stood there shocked. It was no surprise to anyone in the hood that Sierra was on drugs.

Just to see her laying there dead like that was crazy. Damn, I am so sorry to hear that my condolences to you the girls and everyone in her family. Sierra was a good chick. A fly chick as well at one point. She just got caught up and took a wrong turn with those drugs. That shit can happen to anybody if you not strong enough. Beno whispered. He was briefly interrupted when Tony walked up to him.

Tony approached Beno staring directly into his eyes. "Beno! What's shaking my man? How you?" Tony gave Beno a pound and pulled him to the side to talk to him. "You coming to get your shit out of Kema's crib at a time like this? I don't think that would be a great idea at this point and time. As you can see, there are police and detectives all over the fucking place." Tony whispered. He was serious, and you heard it all in his voice.

Letting Beno know that he meant business. "Running up to Kema's crib to grab two kilos of coke right now would be the dumbest mistake of your life." Tony looked around to see who was in the area as he continued his conversation. "Look my man, I suggest you lay low for about a day or two until this shit dies down.

I'll have my girl Mona give you a call tomorrow, so we can figure out a location to meet up for lunch. Sierra is lying dead in the fucking lobby let's think clearly and make it happen on another day." Tony's phone rang while he was having a conversation with Beno. Looking at his phone, he noticed that it was his man Clay who he was trying to meet up with in Harlem before the shit with Sierra popped off.

"Tony, after I called Mona earlier, I also spoke to Kema and she said it was ok for me to come through. I'm not trying to bust nobody's bubble I just came to get what's mines. This shit with Sierra is deep. I can dig what you are telling me though. Ok Tony I got you, Ima lay low for a minute until this shit with Sierra cools off.

I will be back to get my shit from Kema Tony mark my words." Beno pointed at Tony as he let him know he was coming back for his drugs. Tony just nodded him off, so he could get the fuck out of his face. When Beno left, Tony made his way back over to the bench to talk to the girls. "Where the fuck did Kema go?" Tony asked," concerned with his hands in the air.

Mona, Niema and Kizz looked at Tony just as shocked as he was. "I don't know Tony she just got up after her phone rang and walked off without saying a word. She probably went down the hill to get some more liquor for us. Niema replied. Sipping on her Hennessy. "Listen, I must have a word with Kema about Beno and Dirk.

I don't trust those mother fuckers not one bit." All this shit is going to change asap. First, I'm going to hit Sierra's family off with some money, so her mother can bury her daughter. I told Sierra to stay off the pipe. She didn't listen to anyone but that bitch ass crackhead she fucked with. I bet that mother fucker won't even come to pay his respects. He didn't give a fuck about her.

All he did was keep her in the clinic filled with diseases and abortion appointments. He did Sierra dirty for years. I guess you get what you put up with. A man can only do what you let them do. She kept going back to that piece of shit and it killed her. Fucking around with this street shit will have your ass lost if you not strong enough." Tony snarled. The paramedics lifted Sierra's body and placed her into a body bag.

The whole hood watched as the coroner came to pick up Sierra's lifeless body. It was cold as hell up in the projects and the mood was frozen. Kema on the other hand was parked outside of the projects in the backstreets talking to Dirk in a royal blue Benz with tinted windows. Ever since Beno started putting work up at Kema's crib she's been dipping off riding Dirk's dick.

Kema bagged so much drugs up that she came a costume to sniffing cocaine every time she got a chance. Dirk had Kema strung the fuck out fucking her every time he came to pick up a package. Kema would suck him off, get paid and get some extra coke to party with on the low. The Clique had no idea Kema was fucking Dirk. Kema was pissed off by the fact that Dirk got caught with Lori.

She had to talk to Dirk to see what the fuck was on his mind. "Dirk why you do me like that? You could have told me that you were fucking with Tony's girl." Kema squealed. While placing some cocaine onto her fist and snorting it with her left nostril. "Kema, I didn't have to tell you a mother fucking thing. Your job is to bag my shit up and suck my dick good like you been doing. I'll be real funny if I told Tony how good your head game is wouldn't I."

Dirk looked at Kema with a sly smirk on his face. "I don't know what the fuck Tony's problem is, but his bitch chose me. Tony needs to understand that we been running this shit in the hood for years while he was locked down. Now that he's home, he expects everybody to fall back. Who the fuck this nigga thinks he is.

I'm telling you Kema, you better talk to your nigga Tony. That shit he did at the restaurant is far from over. In the meantime, we going to make this paper. Make sure you have your girlfriend Devita meet me, so she could do that job we talked about." Well you are the one who introduced me to her Dirk, now I gotta convince a bitch to suck some dick. Kema snarled. Puffing on Dirk's blunt.

Dirk looked in his rear-view mirror to see if anybody was around his car. "I suggest you get a few alibis together because you and Devita are going to be missing in action." Kema just looked at Dirk with coke on her nose agreeing to everything he had to say. "Make sure you hit me up tomorrow, so I can tell you where to meet me.

I got some high-class ballers who like to fuck and have a good time. These white dudes love to taste black pussy. They are willing to pay top dollar for some freaky chicks." Dirk had plenty hoes making paper for him on the sideline and Kema fell right into his trap. When Kema sniffed cocaine, you could talk her into practically anything. She loved to party, and her level of thinking was like a submissive white chick. "Ok Dirk I will give her a call.

I know she will be down for anything don't worry we will be ready when you call me." Kema wiped her nose and fixed her hair in the mirror. "I gotta get back to the girls before they suspect something is up. I will call you tomorrow." Kema opened the door and walked out of Dirk's car with a big smile on her face.

Dirk pulled off into traffic speeding through Foch to hit the highway. His brother Beno who was waiting in his ride, followed right behind him. Tony thought he had a problem with Dirk over Lori, but he had another problem coming at him in full speed.

Kema was so fucking gullible and skied up that she didn't even see the beef she was causing by fucking with Dirk after she saw him with Lori. Dirk knew he had Kema right where he wanted her.

She was hooked on the coke and the dick and she didn't care if it fucked the relationships up with the people she grew up with. There was a time bomb ticking and she couldn't get out of the barrel that she climbed into.

It was just a matter of time before Tony found out about Kema's moves and she will be very sorry she crossed the one man who had her back and looked out for her since day one. Tony sat down the hill while Mona and the girls went to get some more liquor from the liquor store. Sierra's body was finally taken from the lobby of the building and placed inside of the ambulance.

Tony thought long and hard about all the shit that's happened, and he barely had a chance to breath NYC air. He really had to make a move and knew just what he needed to do. "Hey, what's up my man, talk to me let me know what's popping. I just came home two days ago. I'm in South Side Jamaica Queens right now.

"A lot of shit been happening back to back. It's been one thing after another since I came home, and I only been here two mother fucking days. Listen, my man, I must take a ride up to Harlem to see you soon as possible. Maybe we can meet and have lunch sometime this week." Tony mentioned. Sitting on the bench in the projects.

"Ok, my man. Hit me up in the morning first thing and I'll let you know when and where to meet me." Clay replied. "There's a lot of money to be made Tony you won't want to miss this opportunity." Tony finally gotten a chance to speak to his main man Sammy's nephew Clay. Hanging up the phone, Tony felt real comfortable with his decision to fuck with Clay.

He was feeling the tension of the hood already and it wasn't a good look. He didn't expect to come home to so much drama. Being gone from society for a decade is no joke. It changes you. It's like a culture shock, a feeling of uncertainty. He knew exactly where he was theoretically but mentally he needed to find his way back into the real world.

Everything around him has changed drastically and he just needed a little time to adapt to the new codes of the streets although he remained loyal to his own. There was a new breed in the air and Tony felt that he needed to be very careful about who he trusted at this point. His girl betraying him just made all matters that much worse. Tony had a big vision and he got a great connect that could make him a lot of money.

He needed people around him who had his best interest at heart. He was solid about his decisions and he was ready to put a bullet into anyone who came in between that. After Tony's conversation with Clay, he just sat back with his girls in the basketball court and poured out a little liquor for their childhood friend.

Chapter 3

KEMA

"This shit stings so bad. I should have never let you talk me into this." Kema shouted. Talking to Devita as the tattoo artist finished designing her tattoo. Kema was getting leopard prints tatted on her back right above her ass. She hadn't gotten a tattoo before, so the pain for her was very intense. Kema squirmed at every prick of the needle hitting her skin. She balled up her fist and tried to control the pain. She couldn't wait for the artist to finish so she could use to the bathroom. Her face showed every sign of emotion and frustration as the tattoo artist finished up on her tattoo.

As soon as the artist relieved Kema from her misery, she ran out of the chair straight to the restroom. While using the restroom, Kema pulled out a little bag of cocaine and sniffed it in the bathroom stall. Devita walked into the restroom looking for Kema and knocked on the door so she could join in on the get high. "Damn bitch you practically sniffed up the whole fucking bag.

Devita snarled. Sniffing the rest of the coke inside of the baggie. Shut up Devita, there is plenty more where that came from. Kema smiled. Pulling out another baggie filled with coke. Dirk is going to kill you for taking his coke without permission. Devita whispered. Staring at the coke Kema was holding in her hand. "Yeah, well he gotta catch me first. Kema gloated.

She turned around to show Devita her new tattoo. "How does it look Devita?" Kema asked. Anxiously waiting for a response. "That shit looks sexy, I love it. I think I want to get me one." Devita snorted all the cocaine that was left inside of the baggie and opened the bathroom stall, so she could wash her face and hands.

Kema soon followed flushing the toilet. The room was spinning as Kema looked up at the ceiling. Her eyeballs were wide open, and she felt the numbness of the coke on the tip of her tongue as she licked her fingertips. "That hit of coke just brought my high to a whole new level." Kema whispered. Washing her hands in the sink. Kema's light brown complexion was glowing although she was high as a kite.

She wore a dark brown mini fur with some tight ass black jeans and black timberlands. Her outside appearance hardly matched the flames that were burning from deep within. Kema had been depressed for several months. She was fighting a battle of a lifetime with her mom for custody of her two children who had been taken away from her when she got locked up during a drug sweep a couple years ago.

All the court dates, opinions and guilt took her to a whole new place that kept her numb from all pain. She didn't want to feel like a failure. She did the best she could to be a mother to her son and daughter the first year of their lives, but the struggle between motherhood and the streets took a tole and the streets clearly won the battle.

Kema hadn't seen her daughter in months and she chose to keep it that way as long as her mother fought her for custody. She couldn't understand the consequence of her mistakes and she refused to believe that she was making bad choices. Making that fast paper and keeping up with the jones was all she thought about for the moment. As long as she had her get high, she was a happy camper.

She fixed her lipstick and made sure her nose was straight before she exited the bathroom. Hanging out with Devita every day made everything ten times worse. Devita wasn't very attractive on the inside and her outside appearance was falling apart. Her dark-skinned complexion was flawless, but her face and bone structure were rough and slowly deteriorating from the wear and tear of all the drug use.

Her hair was laced in a long jet-black weave. She had on a red ski jacket and jeans drying her hands in the bathroom twerking to the beat playing in her head. Her bottom line was drugs and she would do every and anything to get it. Kema's whole aura changed once she started fucking with Devita. She was a dark soul. All she did was fuck for money to buy crack. She didn't give a damn about nothing but getting high.

Kema met Devita one day while she was bagging up for Dirk one morning in one of his trap houses on South Road. Devita sold her pussy and head for the bread and would sell her soul if the price is right. Her head game was on point because she didn't have much teeth left in her mouth. All her front teeth rotted up and disappeared from smoking. She was very insecure with low self-esteem.

She never had any real guidance or love from her mother growing up as a kid. Her mother was a crackhead and prostitute tricking for a quick fix ever since she was a small child. The behavior was initially repeated, and the dysfunctional cycle continued. She was raised by a parent who didn't know how to love or teach her children how to love and respect themselves. Devita was blind sighted by a lifestyle that was destroying her wellbeing.

Caught up in the mist of substance abuse and self-hatred. The more Kema met up with Dirk the more she started seeing Devita doing tricks and getting her money sucking and fucking anything that approached her. Dirk started pimping Devita and made a slew of money off her because all she wanted was a place where she could get high.

One-day Dirk had asked Kema if she would assist Devita in getting her some nice stripper outfits for when she worked out on the strip. Dirk put Kema on to all the clients he had who was looking for some young black pussy to fuck. Kema was so naive and gullible that she fell for the okie doke like a young fool.

She agreed to letting Devita stay at her crib, so she could keep tabs on her whenever Dirk needed them to go make some extra money stripping and fucking high-class white-collar clients. These clients paid money for sex and brought large quantities of cocaine for the many affairs they attended with several colleagues. Kema never thought she would get into any shit like this. She was always a down ass street chick until she got caught up with Dirk.

He turned Kema out when he fucked her one night, telling her that she was his main bitch while she sucked his dick in her kitchen. She couldn't resist the urge to fuck him because his money was long, and his dick was so big. She never shared her side hustle with any of the girls in The Clique because she didn't want them to know how far gone she was from sniffing cocaine.

Her habit was spiraling out of control and she thought she had a hold over the drug, but she didn't. After Sierra passed away, her addiction got worse. You would think that a person would learn a lesson from seeing their childhood friend strung out over dosing right before their eyes. In Kema's case it was the total opposite.

Dirk knew for a fact that he could get Kema to do whatever he wanted, and he preyed on her vulnerability. It's funny how a man could just come along and turn your whole life inside out in a split second. Insecurity is a mother fucker. If you don't have a strong mind or confidence within, you can easily fall into any trap waiting to catch you.

There are plenty of men out there who look for women who don't value their self-worth. The crazy thing about it is the man who thinks he can manipulate and control a woman by belittling her; is a loser himself. Weak men cover their worthless tracks through the scars of an insecure woman. Kema had gotten so deep into bagging up drugs, that she lost track of everything else around her. She gave up the goods like it was a pack of cookies in the candy store.

Even Beno got in on fucking Kema and Devita late nights whenever he picked up his work with Dirk on a humble. Kema was fucked up in the head the day she saw Dirk with Tony's girl Lori at the restaurant. She had no idea that he even knew her. Kema started thinking that Dirk had something personal against Tony.

She didn't know how to tell Tony of her actions because she thought he would dead her with the family and their business if she told him, so she just kept her mouth shut. Now she's stuck between fucking Dirk and his clients sniffing cocaine like it's no tomorrow and lying to Tony and her Clique. Kema headed to the mall with Devita so they could get some sexy lingerie and outfits for the clients that Dirk told her about when they were in the projects.

She picked out the trashiest outfits she could find inside of a sex shop downtown in Soho in the village. Both Kema and Devita picked out some guarder belts, whips, handcuffs, hi heels, 10-inch dildos and some anal ease. They grabbed any and everything they thought would turn these rich men on. All the items inside of the sex shop turned Kema on and she couldn't wait to spend her first night as a high-priced hooker.

Driving back from the city high as hell singing to the music in her ride, Kema looked at her phone as it rang sitting inside of the cup holder. She picked the phone up staring at Mona's name on the caller ID. "Oh shit, what the fuck does Mona want. I got too much shit to do today. I hope she doesn't want me to do something for Sierra's funeral. I'm going to hit her back when I finish with Dirk."

Kema sighed. Rolling her eyes as she drove through the mid-town tunnel. Mona on the other hand was left on the other end of the line standing in front of Kema's door. She's been holding a lot of shit in about Kema and she really wanted to know why she's been missing in action for weeks. Mona was vexed and couldn't wait to give Kema a piece of her mind. "This bitch got me fucked up. Why the fuck she not answering the phone knowing we got a funeral to attend this week. I'm telling you Kizz, something is up with Kema.

I got a crazy feeling that Kema is on some other shit. She better get her shit together before she winds up on the other side of The Clique getting her ass kicked." Mona was tight because she hates being ignored by anyone.

She couldn't really pin point what was going on, but she knew that something wasn't right. "Mona don't sweat it. We all going through it right now. Being that Sierra just died the way that she did, I'm sure Kema is just taking this shit just as bad as we are, and everybody mourns differently." Kizz pressed the elevator button as she expressed how she felt about the situation with Kema.

"You may be right Kizz, Ima take that into consideration and lay low for a minute until this shit with Sierra is over. I'm telling you, something ain't right and I'm definitely going to find out what it is believe them apples. Mona looked at Kizz with a funny look up on her face as the elevator door opened.

"What do you think is going on with Kema? Do you think she's fucking around with Dirk? You know Dirk's been spending a lot of time up at her crib. I see his car parked outside of her building practically every other night and not on the days when we are bagging up for him either. I'm not saying that he be with her, but shit who the fuck else is he coming over here to see. My thing is, if he is fucking Kema, how the fuck did he have time to get up with Tony's girl Lori. That nigga doing the most right now."

Kizz bust out laughing as she envisioned some scenarios of Kema and Dirk. "This shit is like a soap opera in these projects and every day is a new episode. I won't be surprised if Kema getting dick down right now.

Shit, nothing doesn't surprise me anymore especially after seeing Sierra laid out in the fucking lobby dead. Sierra is fucking dead! I'm still thinking about her body laying right here in this lobby for hours in the freezing cold. What the fuck! I go to work and come home to see this shit in my hood. Our childhood friend overdosed on dope and crack. How are we supposed to explain this kind of shit to our children? This is the type of shit that you see in the movies not right in front of your face.

We are living in a rough era and we grew up way too fast. We all knew and did things at an early age. When we were supposed to be playing with Barbie dolls, we were out there bagging up kilos of cocaine.

All the money we get from doing this shit is good but the tole it's taking on our lives is the pits. I'm a Correctional Officer now and I still come home and dabble and deal with these drugs because this is all I know. When will the cycle end with living our lives the way that we do. When will the lesson be learned Mona? When we're all dead.

This shit is crazy because we all know the shit we do every day has a consequence, but we wake up every morning and play with the same devil on a different level. Something has got to give Mona or shit is just going to get worse." Kizz just poured her heart out to Mona trying find a better way through all the bullshit that they go through on a day to day basis. Mona listened to her friend talk, but her words went in one ear and right out the other.

Hood Games

"We do this same talk every damn year and we end up right back where we started with piles of money and coke in our faces. Face it Kizz, this is how we do shit, so let's just keep doing what we do and focus on not getting caught. Listen, I don't mean to burst your bubble Kizz, but we got a lot of work coming our way.

Tony just came home, and he done found a whole new connect that's going to make us a ton of money. We can't start thinking like this now, we in too deep. Now that Tony's here, it's a whole new ballgame. We can't just pick up and walk away from this shit, we in this together, we all we got. I know you don't want to lose all the money you stack every month dealing coke to the inmates in prison.

126

That money pays for your son's private school, that brand-new Benz you're driving and those diamond earrings in your ears. Don't front like you don't love all that shit you got. You one of the fly bitches in these projects. Pull yourself together boo, right now is not the time to be doubting any of our moves." Kizz just stared into the wind as Mona continue talking to her.

"We got a way to go before we give up on this lifestyle. Wake up and smell the coffee, it is what it is. Stop beating yourself up about this shit. The best thing we can do for now is the same shit we been doing; hustling and stacking this paper. If we focus on the bigger picture, we won't get so caught up with our emotions.

I know this shit with Sierra is a hard pill to swallow, but Sierra has been sick for a whole fucking decade. We tried our best to get her cleaned up and there was nothing we could have done that would have changed this outcome. The more I think about her the more it pisses me off. By the way this bitch Kema hasn't called me back yet Ima kick her ass when I see her. Mark my words, after Sierra's funeral I'm going to make sure to get to the bottom of Kema's shady moves.

In the meantime, let's go get these flowers and arrangements for the funeral." Mona stated. Lighting up her cigarette. "Listen Mona, we gotta make this quick because I must pick up my son by six o-clock. Oh, let me tell you the good news. Kizz shouted. Smiling from ear to ear.

The head supervisor at my job told me that I got a promotion and they are giving me a fat raise. Buss this though, the Department of Corrections need more officers at Sing Sing Correctional Facility in Ossining New York. Me and two other officers were recommended for the job. That's the prison where Vince is located. I am being promoted and switched over to Sing Sing in two weeks."

Kizz looked at her watch as she continued. "I can't believe that I'm going to be working as a Correctional Officer Supervisor. This shit blew my mind. The commute is perfect too because it's only an hour away." Mona interrupted. "Oh shit! You mean to tell me that you are going to be calling the shots at the same jail that Vince is in.

Who would have thought some shit like this would happen? This shit is fucking crazy. Yes, Kizz, I'm so happy for you. Mona hugged Kizz and congratulated her on her new job offer. Aww man, Ima go see Vince on a visit as soon as you set up shop. Mona whispered. Kizz looked at Mona and winked her eye. "You know what this means right? Kizz asked. Pulling out a cigarette to light it up.

This shit going be ridiculous being around our family in the same prison. I couldn't believe they told me that shit. I'm going to make my rounds in there and get everything situated and then set you up for a visit to come through to see Vince." We gotta keep this shit air tight. I don't want to many people to even know that I work there." Kizz mentioned. Puffing on her cigarette.

"You got that right. Don't tell anyone anything just let a mother fucker assume. It's on and popping. Just let me know when you ready for me to come through and it's on. Mona smiled. As her and Kizz smoked a cigarette together.

"You ready to go and get these arrangements together for Sierra? Mona asked. Fixing her pony tail and putting it into a bun. "I'm really not in the mood for this shit but it must get done. I'm ready when you are Mona." The cold breeze blew in the wind as Kizz and Mona stood silent on the bench in the park with a ton of shit on their minds.

CHAPTER 4

The Funeral

The rain was falling hard from the sky as the wind blew heavy. The day was dreary and somber with stains of grief in the clouds touching every heart in the projects. The snow was now slushy as the rain drops hit the ground. Roses and flowers were everywhere inside of the building on the first floor where Sierra passed away. More than 100 candles were lit up in a row sitting in the lobby from people who paid their respects. Whenever someone dies there is always a new life born. Life has a crazy way of teaching you.

No school or text book could ever teach you life's everyday experiences and lessons. The rains mist flew into Niema's face as she opened her car door. She looked down at her feet as her boots hit the messy slush. Looking up, Niema noticed an ambulance rolling up the hill towards her and Kema's building. Low and behold, there was a young girl who lived on the 5th floor giving birth.

The ambulance arrived just in time to find the baby's head pushing through the pregnant girl's uterus. There was no time to get her to the hospital, so the EMT workers proceeded to deliver the baby right in the hallway of the building. "Oh, my goodness, what a miracle. Life has a funny way of showing up I tell you.

Niema whispered. Watching the young girl being rolled out of the building into the ambulance holding her brand-new baby girl. Niema quickly reached into her purse and grabbed her phone to call Kema so she could come down stairs to see the beautiful new baby that was just born inside of their building. As Kema's phone rang, she stood on her living sofa giving Dirk some head.

While sucking his dick, she got distracted and ran to the kitchen to look at her caller ID. "Yo! Who the fuck is it? Dirk shouted. Standing in the living room with his manhood in his hand. "Oh, my goodness, it's Niema. She just left a message on my phone Dirk she's downstairs." Kema blurted. Running back to the couch butt ass naked.

"So! What the fuck that has to do with me." Dirk snarled. Slapping his penis on Kema's lips. "Damn, Dirk. Did you hear what I said? Niema is downstairs and who knows who she's with; they might come up here any minute and I do not want her or anyone else to see you here with a hard dick standing in the middle of my living room.

"So, you mean to tell me that I gotta get dressed and sit on your couch with blue balls because your friends are coming up in here. Bitch you got me all the way fucked up. You better come jump on this dick." Dirk grabbed Kema by her ass and threw her onto the couch then fucked her doggy style smacking her on her ass as hard as he could. "Bitch, don't ever tell me to leave without giving me what's mines."

Kema moaned softly as Dirk pulled on her hair. Dirk was turned on by Kema's thick thighs and huge breasts. He couldn't control the urge to cum all over her tits. When Dirk released his lust all over Kema's breasts, there was a loud knock at her door. "Knock… knock… knock. "Oh shit! See, I fucking told you they were coming up here.

Damn, Dirk, look at this shit. Kema looked up at Dirk with an attitude pushing him off her running into the bathroom so she could hurry up and clean herself up. As Niema knocked again, she started yelling Kema's name from the other side of the door. "Kema wake up, we know you in there open up this door. Kema quickly washed her ass and tits and yelled.

"Just a minute." She rushed as she pulled up her pants while running into the living room. Once she reached the living room, Dirk was still standing there but naked with one sock on. "Yo! What the fuck are you doing, get dressed. You know what, forget it we don't got time for all this shit."

Kema grabbed all of Dirk's clothes and took him by the hand pulling him towards the back of the apartment into her bedroom and put him inside of her closet. "Dirk, just stay in here until they leave okay. I have no idea who is at the door and I really don't feel like explaining this shit to nobody." Kema left Dirk speechless with his eyes and mouth wide open as she shut the closet door in her room. Opening the front door, Kema is greeted by Niema, Kizz, Mona, Kai and Tony.

"Damn, it took you long enough. What the fuck was you doing in here sucking dick or something?" Tony laughed. Staring at Mona like she was crazy as they all looked around the apartment before sitting down in the living room. "Mona shut up, ain't nobody sucking no damn dick.

What are you all doing here so early? Sierra's funeral isn't until later." Kema asked. Scared to death thinking that Dirk was going to walk out into the living room any second. "The real question here is. What the fuck is going on with you? You've been missing in action lately and I just want to know who the fuck is occupying your time when we are calling you and coming up to your crib. None of the girls heard from you in days. A lot of shit just not adding up.

Ever since Sierra died you have been ghost. Whenever Dirk's car is parked in the projects your ass is nowhere to be found. Are you fucking with this nigga or something? Mona asked. Staring at Kema in the living room. "She's got a point though Kema. I mean, this mother fucker done fucked my girl, and he's talking mad shit about me in these streets.

I know you not stupid enough to go against the grain and fuck with this nigga after everything that just happened. Is his stash still here or what? Did you give it back to him yet? I haven't heard from Beno since the night of Sierra's death." Tony asked Kema a slew of questions trying to get to the bottom of his suspicion. "Yes, Tony, his stash is still here. I haven't heard from Dirk or Beno since they were in the projects the night we found out about Sierra.

I don't know why you all are on my back like I'm a kid or something. I didn't do shit wrong and I'm not fucking with Dirk on a sexual level. It's strictly business with Dirk. We bag up his shit, get paid and part ways that's it. Kema looked at Tony straight in the eyes lying through her teeth. Knowing damn well that Dirk was sitting right up in her closet.

"So, where you been all this time I needed you to help me with the arrangements for Sierra. I couldn't reach you all weekend. What the fuck is that about?" Mona asked. Looking at Kema with a disgusted look. Kema just stared back at Mona not saying a word to her. Suddenly, there was a loud thump coming from the back of Kema's apartment. "Yo! What the fuck was that? Tony asked.

"Is somebody here with you Kema? Kema stared at Tony with a stupid look up on her face. Tony got up and walked his way to the back of Kema's apartment. He checked the bathroom, and no one was in there. He then looked straight to the back towards Kema's bedroom. Tony walked into a room right across from Kema's and saw Devita sleeping in the bed. He just stared at Devita as she slept with a tank top and thong on staring at her sagging tits thinking to himself. *"Who the hell is that ugly bitch?"*

He closed the door softly and proceeded to Kema's room. Opening the door, Tony looked around and noticed a man's jacket and boots in Kema's room. Once he stepped inside, he could feel the presence of someone in the room.

"Yo! Kema. Who are you shacking up with? Where your boo at? He left his boots behind." Tony chuckled. Looking at all Kema's perfume and make up on top of her dresser. There were also four big stacks of hundred-dollar bills, twenties and fifties inside of her drawer wrapped in rubber bands. The drawer was slightly open as Tony peeked inside seeing the stash that he just asked Kema about. "Get the hell out of my room Tony and stop being so nosey."

Kema stormed into her room shouting at Tony for him to get out and respect her privacy. She was scared to death looking at the closet while trying to push Tony back into the hallway. "Get the fuck out of here Kema, I'm not going nowhere. Whose money you holding?

This is a big wad of cash and I know this shit ain't yours." Tony reached inside of the drawer, took off the rubber bands and started counting the money in front of Kema as she grabbed at it pleading for him to give the money back to her. Mona and the girls entered the room as Kema and Tony tussled around the room for the cash.

Dirk could see everyone who was inside of the room through the cracks inside of the closet and he was pissed off knowing that Tony was in plain sight fucking with his stash. Dirk sat there for a minute ready to open the closet door, when his cell phone began to ring. The ringing of the phone sounded all around the room. Everyone who was in the room froze to see where the ringing was coming from.

"It's coming from over there." Mona shouted. Pointing at the closet. Dirk grabbed his phone and quickly ended the ringing; but it was too late. Kizz opened the closet door to see Dirk sitting inside butt ass naked. "Yo! What the fuck." Kizz jumped back a little startled by what she saw. "You are a lying ass bitch!"

Mona shouted. Shaking her head from side to side staring at Kema with disgust. As Dirk lifted himself up to put his shirt on, Tony came and pulled him from out of the closet. "What the fuck are you doing in here hiding like a little bitch and why the hell are you naked? Tony asked. Holding Dirk's money in his hand. "Look, you haven't been in these streets in years and now you want to come up in here questioning me like you're running shit.

I don't gotta tell you a mother fucking thing. Now give me my money and get the fuck out of my face." Dirk proceeded to get dressed putting his shirt over his head and pulled up his pants. Mona and the girls couldn't believe what they were seeing. Kema's heart was in her knee caps shook not knowing what was about to happen. Dirk swung at Tony once he put on his pants and missed as he continued to grab for his money. It was on and popping up in Kema's apartment. Kai and Kizz held Kema on the bed while Niema Mona and Tony started fucking Dirk up.

Dirk started swinging back and punched Mona in her mouth. Tony then pulled out his pistol and hit Dirk in the face with it knocking him down to the floor. Mona's mouth was bleeding as she watched Dirk fall to the floor.

Tony jumped on top of Dirk pistol whipping his face to a bloody pulp. Kema was screaming as Tony went into a rage. "This is my mother fucking projects; don't you ever forget that shit. Tony kept swinging the gun on Dirk with every word he spoke trying to kill him. Dirk cried and uttered as his body shook from the beating. "Tony get off him you're going to kill him, stop it Tony, please stop." There was no stopping Tony he kept beating Dirk with the gun until Dirk stopped moving. Dirk was dead, and blood was everywhere. All over the floor and Tony's clothes.

Kema's friend Devita ran into the room and started screaming. Mona and Niema quickly grabbed her and covered up her mouth so she could shut up. They both brought her into the room and tied her body up to the chair.

Devita cried uncontrollably telling Kema that she was going to call the police if they didn't let her go. Mona ran to the stereo to turn on the music. She turned the volume up as loud as she could so no one from outside of the apartment could hear what was going on. "Bitch, you threatening me? Do you know who the fuck I am? Who the fuck is this bitch Kema.? Tony shouted. Pointing his fingers on Kema's forehead. "I met her through Dirk we were working together for him. Kema replied. Crying her eyes out.

"Listen, I will do anything you say please just let me go. If you do anything to me my brother is a police officer and he will find you." Devita screamed. "Bitch you think I give a fuck about your brother or the police. I will fucking kill you bitch. Tony pointed his gun at her ready to pull the trigger.

"Fuck you mother fucker you don't fucking scare me. Your ass is going to jail soon as my brother finds out about this." Mona and Niema just looked at each other and the rest of the girls got up off the bed and started beating the shit out of Devita. The Clique was whipping Devita's ass while Kema cried in her bedroom. Devita managed to untie the knot from her hands and started fighting back. She then grabbed Niema by the hair trying to scratch her eyes out. She held Niema's hair around her fist and would not let go.

Niema started screaming trying her best to get Devita off her. Kizz, and Mona started punching Devita in her face and head repeatedly, when Kai walked up and kicked her in her chest. Devita let go of Niema's hair and flew to the floor.

Mona pushed Kizz out of the way and started stomping Devita out kicking her all in her grill. She was fuming and couldn't see anything else but blood in her eyes. Kema screamed as Mona stomped Devita in the face. Suddenly, Devita started shaking uncontrollably as her body went into shock. She suddenly stops shaking laying on the floor with her eyes wide open. Devita was dying right in front of their eyes. The music was blasting while everybody in the room was stuck. "Look what you made me do.

I should put a bullet in your ass for lying to me, stupid bitch. All this shit could have been avoided if you were keeping it real from jump. You up in here fucking and sucking on the same nigga who sleeping with my ex and planning to go to war with me.

How the fuck am I supposed to trust you after this. You lucky you apart of the family Kema; I'm about ready to shoot you right where you stand. Get the fuck up and find some towels and bleach so we can clean this shit up. We got a fucking funeral to go to today and we are sitting up in here with two dead bodies." Dirk and Davita was dead and Tony was fuming as he and the girls sat in Kema's apartment cleaning up the mess she created.

*****

"I can't believe my baby is gone. She had her whole life ahead of her. Oh, lord please give me the strength to bury my baby girl this morning. Sierra's mother cried as she prepped the potato salad. The eggs were boiling in the pot along with ten huge potatoes.

Sierra's cousin sat at the table peeling fresh string beans. Aunt Betty I am so sorry you must bury your daughter today. She was such a beautiful young lady. It is a crying shame that my beautiful cousin had to go out the way that she did. I love her to death aunt Betty. Whatever you need from me please don't hesitate to ask. Sierra's cousin Chinky sat at her aunts table helping her prepare the menu for Sierra's funeral.

It was 10 AM in the morning and all Sierra's mother wanted to do is rest but she just couldn't stop cooking for her only daughter's funeral. She was so tired. Her eyes were puffy from crying all night and her body was drained. She was trying to find the strength from within to move forward. The task was so overwhelming because she just lost her son a year ago who died of Cancer. The agony was taunting at her heart.

The pain of losing a child is the worst thing that could possibly happen to a parent. Her mother was in so much pain. She had nothing else to live for. She spent the last five years of her life fighting the battle of Cancer with her son to turn around and face the death of her daughter. "It wasn't easy dealing with a child on drugs you know. My Sierra was a fucking trip. If I could, I would have nailed my purse to my hand to keep her from stealing money out of it."

Betty laughed. Seasoning four pans of turkey wings as she talked about the times she shared with her daughter. "That Sierra sure knew how to make me laugh, especially if I was mad at her. She would jump in front of me shaking her little skinny high yellow ass until I laughed that's my baby. Betty smiled. Looking at her daughter's picture in a frame.

"There's going to be so many people at the funeral. We are going to have to cook for about sixty people. I will pick up some fried chicken from Popeyes to save us some time on all this cooking. Myrtle from building two said she will bake two cakes and make some peach cobbler. I sure will be glad when this day is over, so I can mourn in peace." Sierra's mother mixed the ingredients for the potato salad and stirred it inside of a large bowl.

Suddenly there was a knock-on Betty's door. "Just a second." Betty shouted. As she finished stirring up her potato salad. "Who on earth could it be this early?" Betty asked. Clenching her robe while running towards the door. Looking through the peephole, Sierra's mother noticed that it was Mona at the door.

"Mona. What on earth are you doing over here this early? We won't be meeting up until later this evening. I got my yams going, my baked mac and cheese, and my turkey wings, the food is going to be out of sight. Come on in here baby." Betty hugged Mona as she walked into her apartment telling her of all the great dishes that she was cooking for her daughter. "Hello Ms. Betty, I just came over to ask you if you had a couple of towels I could barrow.

Niema's friend Cookie came over with her new baby and pooped all over her brand-new couch. We are trying to get the stains out now, but we ran out of fresh towels. I think we may need some more bleach as well. If you have some that would be great."

Mona mentioned. Trying not to look like a nervous wreck. "Why sure dear I have plenty of clean towels and plenty of bleach. I buy in bulk you know." Sierra's mother answered. She went into her room to retrieve the clean towels out of her closet. "I will give you some paper towels and tissue as well. You ladies must keep your house loaded with this stuff always, it is very important because you never know when you might run into an emergency. Ok now, this should be enough to clean everything right on up."

Betty handed Mona six large towels, two rolls of paper towel, toilet tissue and a big bottle of bleach. "I hope everything comes out of the couch; that is a nightmare. Tell Tony he is a blessing for helping me pay for the funeral and let me know if you need anything else dear."

Leaving Betty's apartment, Mona just stood in the hallway and cried. She could not believe the trouble she was in. As she made her way to the elevator, she wiped her tears and got herself together. "Hey Clay, I'm in a real jam my man. I'm going to need your assistance asap. You think you could meet me in Baisley projects in about an hour. Tony was sweating bullets while he talked to Clay over the phone.

I'm telling you it's an emergency can't tell you shit over this phone right now. "Ok Tony, I will be over there in an hour. See you soon." Clay hung up with Tony and headed to the highway to make it over to Queens from Harlem. So many things ran through his mind as he thought of how nervous Tony sounded over the phone just a minute ago.

He just hoped for the best and headed over there to see what the fuck was going on. When Mona got back, she went straight to the sink to soak two of the towels that Ms. Betty gave her in hot water. After the towels were steaming hot, she poured bleach over top of them. Mona and The Clique wiped that whole apartment spotless. They cleaned the kitchen the living room and the bathroom. Tony made sure everything in both bedrooms were clean as well.

All the blood that was on the floor was now gone and Dirk and Devita's body were wrapped up in carpet sitting inside of Kema's closet. "I know this is some heavy shit to swallow, but we can all get through this shit together. If we just stick together and keep our mouths shut everything will be okay. "Listen Kema, we had to kill that bitch Devita.

She was running off with her mouth about the police and right now I'm not going back to jail for no fucking body. After that mother fucker Dirk punched Mona in her mouth; I just lost it. I am fucking furious with you for fucking with that nigga. Right now, is not the time to be thinking about any of this shit. We all need to be on the same page and keep it that way. If Beno calls any one of you, you tell that mother fucker that you haven't seen or heard from Dirk or Devita in a couple of days. I don't care what he says you just stick to your guns and don't say a mother fucking word about this shit ever.

I'm telling you Kema, you better keep your fucking mouth shut or you're going to have a lot of fucking problems. Your loyalty lies with us and I suggest you pull yourself together and act like you are a part of this family.

Dirk asked for this shit the minute he started fucking Lori. I told that mother fucker he was going to get it. I'm glad he's out of the fucking picture. Now I can finish where I left off without having this crab ass mother fucker to worry about." Tony just sat on Kema's couch counting the money that he took from her drawer. Kema didn't have nothing to say to Tony. She was just happy that she wasn't joining the bodies that were sitting in her closet.

"Tony counted $35,000. Here's a little chump change for your worries. Tony gave each girl $5,000 and he kept $10,000 for himself. "The things that go on in these projects I tell you; a mother fucker could write a book about the shit we go through true story."

Tony mentioned. Staring at his phone as it rang in his hand. Clay finally made it to the projects and met up with Tony. When he knocked on the door, everybody remained quiet until Tony signaled them that everything was cool. When Clay walked into Kema's room and saw the two bodies inside of the closet, he just looked at Tony dumb founded. "Yo! What the fuck is wrong with you Tony. You just came home, and you got a body count.

You crazier than a mother fucker. You can't just go around killing mother fuckers because their getting on your nerves." Clay laughed. Sipping on his orange juice. Him and Tony sat down in the kitchen and figured out a way to get the bodies out of the apartment without anyone noticing their moves.

It's going to be a crazy winter with all this heat you're bringing in. I'm a little impressed that no one heard this shit going down. We are going to have to leave the bodies here for the day until later tonight. I don't think it would be smart for us to take these bodies out of here right now in broad day light. There are a lot of nosey mother fuckers that be watching your moves just for the hell of it.

I know a few dudes who could get the job done for a good price. In the meantime, you all gotta lay low and act like nothing ever happened over here. Clay quoted Tony a price for him to get the bodies out of the apartment. They both agreed to take care of everything later that night when everyone was at Sierra's gathering. Once a bad choice is made, everything in your life could change in a quick second.

Shit is crazy how you could be chilling one minute and then sitting on two bodies the next. Tony's mind was blown about all the shit he has endured in a weeks' time. Hey, shit happens. You either get with the program or get dealt with and that is just what The Clique did. All the girls went over to Mona's crib after they got something to wear and picked up some pizza from Margherita's.

"Yo! I think I am going to have nightmares about this shit for a few weeks. Whenever Tony is in town somebody is laid the fuck out somewhere. Kai giggled. Eating her pizza with the girls in Mona's house. Yeah, but you can't blame him. Dirk is the one who was sitting up in Kema's closet naked with an attitude. If anything, he should have been apologizing to Tony for what he did.

Kema I cannot believe you were fucking Dirk all this time. Girl, you are lucky Tony didn't kill your ass. Why didn't you tell me you were fucking with him? What's wrong with you? What if Dirk had his gun on him? It could have been Tony in your apartment dead all because of your careless choices. Mona expressed how things could have gone terribly wrong had it been the other way around.

"I'm so sorry for everything. I didn't know how bad this situation was until it was too late. I was so scared to talk to you all about Dirk because I was afraid that Tony wouldn't fuck with me anymore. When I found out about Lori, the shit got even worse. I was already caught up in a situation that I couldn't dig myself out of.

Right now, I am just wondering how to deal with Beno. I know he is going to be looking for his brother and his money. It's just a matter of time until he starts hitting up my phone. I would change my number, but I don't want him to think anything fishy is going on – on my end. Ima have to let him know that Dirk took his stash and bread and went on a call tricking with Devita." Kema couldn't even eat sitting in the chair at the table nervous as hell.

"Oh, you mean to tell me Dirk was a pimp too. Niema laughed. scraping the cheese off her pizza with her finger. "Nothing shocks me anymore I swear." Well I am glad that we all are okay and that no one heard that commotion over at your crib.

Tony and Clay will get the bodies out and everything will be fine. I pray that we can all get through this shit without getting caught up. Kai whispered. Looking at her girls at the table. "You are right about that Kai. We got enough shit to worry about. That damn Tony is so fucking hot headed. Once he gets mad there is no stopping him. What we need to do is figure out our alibies once the shit hits the fan. I be damned if I'm sitting up in anybody's jail over this bullshit.

The Clique were all in agreeance with Kizz as they figured out what their stories were during the times of Devita and Dirk's murder. "I swear we been watching too much law & order, we got this shit down pack." Mona whispered. Walking towards the kitchen. "You better believe that I won't say a damn thing, this secret is going to my fucking grave.

Mona poured herself a big glass of Moet and guzzled it down with one gulp. Tony had gotten up to call Clay, so he could arrange the time to meet during the funeral services. The mood at Mona's crib was on edge. Everyone in Mona's apartment were still in shock. It was a long day and they had a whole night ahead of them. The Clique cleaned themselves up well and got dressed in their finest clothes to send their friend Sierra off in style. Sierra's funeral was packed.

The whole entire hood attended and paid their respects. Sierra's mom was comforted with flowers gifts and given plenty of money to bury her only daughter. There's only one thing good about a funeral, it will always bring people together in the same room whether they speak or not. The Clique sent their friend off in style with a murder on their hands.

CHAPTER 5

The Connect

The snow was finally melting as the cold air crept through the night. It was cold as shit! The streets in Harlem were ghost due to the frigid temperature. There was a middle-aged woman standing on the corner of 125th street and Morningside with a thin windbreaker on with no hat or gloves shivering but still bold enough to ask for a dollar as she opened the door for every customer that entered or exited the diner. The air was so brisk that you could see the frost exiting the nostrils. Clay loved the cold weather and he was dressed accordingly with his navy-blue Hilfiger down coat, navy-blue timberlands and jeans. As he entered the diner, he gave the woman who opened the door for him a ten-dollar bill.

As soon as the woman looked at the money she let go of the door and scooted down the street to chase her habit. Clay sat down at M&G Diner to get a bite to eat while he waited on his man Tony to slide through. "Excuse me Miss. May I place an order please. I'll have some grits and eggs scrambled with cheese with some fried cat fish to go with it. You can give me an orange juice to go with that also thank you." As Clay placed his order, Tony was driving through 125th street blasting Padlock- By Gwen Guthrie.

"Boom Ba Doom Boom Badoomp!" Tony just bopped his head to the beat as he found a parking space across the street from the diner. He had an old soul and he listened to all the old school jams that he grew up on when he rolled through the streets with his uncle Vince.

Clay could see Tony sitting in his car on the phone as he skimmed through the daily newspaper. "Hey baby! You pick the craziest times to call me Mona." Tony smiled. Turning down the music. "I'm out here in Harlem making a move or two with my man Clay. I will hit you back a little later when I'm done." Tony spoke to Mona for a brief minute before he exited the car. "Ok Tony, be careful out there, love you madly." Tony smiled to the sound of Mona's sexy voice. "I love you back Mona." Hanging up the phone, he made his way across the street and into the diner.

The smell of baked mac and cheese and smothered chicken with onions hit his nostrils as soon as he opened the door. *"Damn it smells good as hell up in here."* Tony thought. Walking up to Clay's table.

"Hey, my man. What's happening?" Tony gave Clay a side hug and a dap before he sat down to join him. "I can't call it, same shit different day just chasing this paper my man." Clay replied. The waitress brought him his food and it looked delicious. "May I take your order Sir?" The waitress asked with a grin. "Yes, you may. I'll take a flame broiled steak well done, with lots of onions fried on the side, some home fries and some scrambled eggs with cheese. You can bring me an ice-cold water to wash it down with thank you."

Tony replied with a smile. "This was supposed to be the original meeting for the two of us. Something nice and casual where we could discuss money, bricks and numbers. Now we are sitting in here like two hitmen on the lookout. What a difference a day makes."

Clay mentioned.   Stirring at his grits.   "I respect your gangster Tony, but you are one crazy mother fucker."   He laughed as he poured a shot of vodka into his orange juice. "Aww, man, I really didn't expect that shit to go down the way it did Clay word! This dude Dirk came at me crazy and then he punched Mona in her mouth.

When he did that, I just lost it, true story. I want to thank you from the bottom of my heart for coming through for me the way that you did. You really didn't have to do that shit. I owe you one, big time. If it wasn't for you, shit, I would be sitting up in somebody's jail cell counting sheep. Honest to god, it's been a crazy month all together. Soon as I get out the joint I'm getting cheated on, knocking mother fuckers out and catching bodies all in one fucking week.

Who the fuck goes through shit like this? I really can't call it. I envisioned a romantic week with my ex girl Lori, a nice dapper don welcome home party from all my people and to just come back to major love, money making moves, happy places and spaces. That's how it was supposed to go down. But you know shit don't always go according to planned.

That nigga Dirk asked for this shit. If you fuck with me, be prepared for the wrath that's coming your way. The choice is always yours. Anybody who got dealt with on Sammy and Vince's watch deserved that shit and had it coming full force. Tony thanked the waitress as she brought him his food. "Listen my man, I don't even want to talk about this shit right now word.

Bad enough we just buried one of our childhood friends, this shit right here got me ready to take a hit of that coke my damn self. I'll just stick to the Henny and coke for now though." Tony pulled out a nip of Hennessy from his jacket pocket and took it to the head. Clay interrupted and mentioned that they had to get to work asap.

"Listen my man, we gotta get to work like yesterday. All this extra shit, lets dead the shit right now as we speak. I only did the shit I did for you on the strength of my uncle Sammy. He is like a father to me and every time I got up with him he had nothing but great things to say about you and he always mentioned that you were very loyal to your team. Now, I know you were fucked up over the shit that happened with Sierra; but you can't let that shit stop your hustle.

We all do a lot of fucked up shit, but no one makes you put the coke in your nose, shoot that dope into your veins or raise that pipe to your lips. That chick Devita was a dead woman walking. It was just a matter of time before she got caught up just the way Sierra did. That bitch was all over South Road sucking all kinds of dick.

I wouldn't be surprised if she had the monster. Her days were numbered just by the way she moved. That night me and my partner took those bodies out of Kema's crib, we drove way out to New Jersey Shore in the boondocks, set them both on fire and dumped their bodies into the river. Whatever remains that are left, will never trace back to you. Shit, I don't even think the police would even figure out who they are. "Ashes to ashes and dust to dust."

Those mother fuckers were burnt to a crisp." Clay continued as he nibbled on a piece of fish. "It's crazy the way it happened, but you've got to protect yourself by any means. In life, it's always about decisions and choices. Let's put some of this shit that just happened in the wind and focus on the bigger picture. I want you to meet a great friend of mines named Princess'.

This chick is a straight beast. She's Italian and black with a banging body. Very beautiful woman. She owns two strip clubs and a beauty salon out in Long Island. She got a heavy list of clients that buys weight from State to State. Just because she's a female, don't get it twisted; her entourage if crazy. She's got a lot of heavy hitters who roll with her and got her back one hundred percent.

Her father runs everything, but he lets his daughter Princess call the shots with all major connections. She got these mob bosses eating out of her hand filling their parties and secret locations with exotic women, on some fantasy island, dreams of pleasure and sex getaways. Her rolodex is filled with rich men who love high priced hoes that get the job done. Her clientele is over the top.

Some of the biggest mob bosses and drug kingpins conduct business with her on the regular. Her hoes are paid lovely fucking these rich millionaire execs for checks. These doctors and lawyers snort more coke than these crackheads out in these streets. This is where we come in at on the job.

The traffic be heavy and two men such as ourselves are needed to hold shit down moving this weight and money to all the major connects in all the boroughs of New York City. Ima tell you right now, Princess is pretty as fuck, and she likes getting her way with men such as yourself. I advise you to keep everything on a professional level if you want to be respected and carry this business for the long hall. Business is never personal, remember that.

Let's just do our jobs well, stack this paper and keep it moving. Clay just explained some factors of the business he wanted to include him in on. "Hey Clay, I remember you telling me a lot about this dude name Frederico when you wrote me a while back when I was in the pen.

You didn't emphasize to much about the connect but I was just curious if he has his hands tied into all of this. Tony asked while eating his food. Clay had Tony's undivided attention as he drizzled his onions onto his steak. "Oh, yeah, I was just about to get to that. There's some Guido Italian cats that I need to set a meeting with that push weight with Frederico.

Rico, is Princess's father. He got a ton of warehouses out in Long Island and out here where I run shit in Spanish Harlem that Distributes cocaine, dope and prescription pills pushing through the boroughs of New York to Atlanta. I need someone like you to come in and hold shit down on some real boss shit.

Your resume runs deep since the days that Vince was home and I roll with nothing but the best." Clay had nothing but respect for Tony and he wanted to make him his new partner in crime. Tony was flattered by the offer and gladly accepted. Being that Clay was Sammy's nephew, just made the deal that much sweeter. Tony missed the shit out of both Sammy and Vince.

When he first got locked up, he had a hard time dealing with Sammy's death. He had many lonely nights thinking of ways that he could have saved his life. It was emotionally and mentally draining going from living the good life to dwelling in a jail cell. When your world changes drastically you are faced with reality.

You must detach your mind from the element and elevate your spirit from within to be able to function in an unstable environment. The strength a man endures while he is in prison is incredible. For the most part, Tony was just happy that he made it back in one piece. After Clay and Tony wrapped up their meeting, they both agreed to take a ride out to Long Island.

Clay wanted to put Tony on about the heists coming up, but he chose to mention that later. He knew that Tony was the best man for the job. His instincts had a great feeling about him. Clay was a professional at opening safes and locks. He could pop the combination to damn near anything.

Every month he and his crew surfed the neighborhoods for millionaires who lived in mansions out in the suburbs making a fortune off their jewels, money, electronics, anything worth value was taken on a heist. The mission is making money. There's no in between when it comes to that green. Violence is never the motive but if it presented itself it's killed or be killed. "Rico is a very dangerous man and his jobs are fit for a savage. He studies his clients and customers who visits the strip clubs and sex houses and makes his mark on the ones he wants robbed.

The game was played in various ways when it came to that paper. Only some chosen few knew the details of Rico's business." Clay pushed his plate to the side as he continued.

"This meeting was a success and Rico is going to be pleased to know that you are now on board. We have a lot of jobs coming up with large amounts of money to be made. Believe me you would not be sitting with me if you weren't a real mother fucker. Your reputation in these streets is what attracted me to you. I've been hearing your name ring bells for a long time. You're going to make a lot of money with us Tony. Now, let's head over to Long Island and see what's popping at the strip club. Tony and Clay left the diner and headed towards his car.

He then drove around the corner through the back streets on 126th street to Clay's truck. Clay opened his car and went into the glove compartment to grab some VIP passes.

He handed one to Tony and told him to follow him, so he could meet his new connect. The infamous mob boss Frederico and his daughter Princess.

Rico knew Tony was coming to meet him and by Clay's description, he was pleased to introduce Tony into the family and welcome him to his first heist.

CHAPTER 6

THE CLIQUE

The water ran inside of the sink with bubbles and suds rising to the top, while Niema lathered the sponge with soap. While washing the dishes, she looked around the kitchen for Clorox, so that she could clean off the counter tops as soon as she finished washing her last plate. Her mood was tense as her eyes watered up with tears. The smell of the bleach was strong as she scrubbed the counter tops wiping every surface clean. She was fully dressed in her black leather pants, a nice blue blouse and suede boots that gotten wet from the rain when she dropped her son off at daycare.

She was very careful not to spill any of that bleach onto her nice outfit. It was 9AM in the morning and she hadn't been to work in two days. She thought about the lies she was going to create when she got ready to call her boss. *"Everything in this house has to be perfect."* Niema thought. Looking around the apartment. She was a nervous wreck re-rinsing out the rag so that she could wipe down the table in the dining room.

She quickly cleaned the bathroom sink and ran into the bedroom to make sure that the bed was made. Fluffing up the pillows, Niema's cell phone rang. She continued straightening the sheets before she ran to answer the phone. "Hello. She answered huffing and puffing trying to catch her breath. "Hey girl, this is Kizz. What's up boo? Kizz whispered. Smiling on the other end of the line. Hey Kizz. What's up? Niema hardly got the last word out tired and out of breath from running all over the house.

Damn! What you doing fucking bitch? Why you sound like that? Kizz laughed as she listened to Niema who was still breathing hard. "No, I'm not fucking, I'm in here trying to clean up this apartment before this mother fucker Nitty get in here. You already know how he is with his OCD acting ass. Niema rolled her eyes to the thought of Nitty walking into her crib at any moment.

"Oh yes that mother fucker off the chain. He need some counseling with the type of shit he got going on." Niema laughed at Kizz as she continued. "No, I'm serious, that dude right there is bugged out. "Hold on for a minute Niema. "Kizz placed her phone into her pocket, so she could take in the next visitor who came to visit an inmate at her job. The phone wasn't supposed to be on her person while working, but she didn't give two fucks.

The young girl who came in on the visit brought her ID and paperwork up to the front desk. Kizz retrieved the paperwork and pointed her in the direction of the lockers so she could get a key to place all her items inside before going on the visit. Kizz wrote down the visitor's name placed her ID inside of the container and then grabbed her phone, so she could finish her conversation she was having with her best friend.

"Yeah girl, that was a visitor, had to handle my business. Kizz giggled. Listening to Niema laughing at her on the other end. "What's on the agenda after work, I'm trying to go out tonight and have a little fun. I'm tired of sitting up in this house like a fucking maid." Soon as Niema finished her sentence, her boyfriend Nitty knocked on the door.

"Oh shit! That nigga at the door right now. Ima have to call you back girl, hit you up later. "She whispered goodbye to her friend, then she put her phone on the dining room table. "One second!" She shouted. Running to the door. Opening the door, Nitty pushed his way through carrying two big shopping bags from the foot locker. "You see me with all these bags and you gonna just stand right there in the way."

Nitty went straight into the living room with his bags and put them on the couch. "Why was the top lock on the door Niema? You never lock that lock. You did the same shit the last time I left out." Nitty walked over to the table to empty out his pockets. He sat his phone, his money and his keys down then walked back into the living room.

"Oh, my goodness, I just opened up the door baby that's all. Why you gotta start? It's too early for this right now." Niema whispered. Staring at the shopping bags that were sitting on the couch. Nitty walked in beefing. He had a knack for starting shit for no damn reason. No matter what Niema did for him, he always found something about her to destroy and dismantle. It was all about him. He was a control freak and wanted everything his way.

"What the fuck is that smell, damn. I can't even take my clothes out of the bag until that smell airs up out of here." Nitty walked over to the windows in the living room and opened them up for the air to come through. He then went into the bedroom and did the same thing. "I made you some breakfast Nitty, it's on the stove.

I can fix you a plate if you like." Niema tried her best to please her man, but everything she said and did was a problem. She was so nervous tip toeing through the apartment trying not to upset him. Standing in the kitchen, she began praying to herself for a good day. She was so tired of being mentally and physically abused. She met Nitty after she broke up with her baby father.

She fell for him after he wined and dined her treating her like royalty when they first met. Her baby father was the only man she ever truly loved until Nitty came along and swept her off her feet. She would do anything to make him happy.

In the beginning of their relationship, he was very charming and respectful until the day he showed his true colors and started whipping her ass every night.

Niema made Nitty a plate of scrambled eggs, bacon and French toast. She then rinsed out a fork from the dish rack and brought the food over to the dining room table. Nitty went over to the table and sat down to eat. He checked the food thoroughly before biting into his bacon. "This shit is fucking cold. How are you going to serve me some cold breakfast? Didn't I tell you to have my food hot and ready for me when I walk through the door.

He threw the plate so hard that it flew across the table and hit Niema in the chest. The food fell onto Niema and the table and the plate fell on the floor and broke. Nitty then got up and grabbed Niema by her pony tail and put her head to the food making her eat the bacon. "Is that shit hot to you? Eat it bitch. Eat it.

He repeated his words as he continued to force Niema's head down. Niema tried to get out of his grip but he was too strong. Nitty then lifted her head and started punching her in the face repeatedly. "The next time I tell you to do something bitch; I want the shit done. Now, pick this shit up before I make you eat it of the floor." Niema quickly ran to the broom and started sweeping all the food and broken pieces of the plate into the dustpan.

She cried softly as Nitty went to sit down on the couch trying on his new kicks. She couldn't believe that she fell for a man who treated her the way that he did. She was so afraid to tell anyone what she was going through because she thought they would judge her and make her feel even worse.

She was in the mix of losing her job by taking off from work trying to hide all the bruises she gets from getting her ass whipped. The decision to stay in an abusive relationship is never a great outcome. When a woman loves a man who beats her, she is choosing that man over herself, her children, her family, and anyone who cares for her.

Many say a woman is insecure who stays with a man that physically abuses her, but don't see the qualities of the woman before that woman was chosen by a weak man. Many men who lack the love stability and confidence within themselves tend to look for women who are pretty, confident, independent, well manured, and willing to do great things for the love of their relationship.

These qualities that a man sees in a woman that is so beautiful and delightful when he first meets her; slowly breaks down as he beats her and mentally drains her into a world full of hurt, confusion, insecurity, and pain. He strips her from the woman she once believed in and brings her to a woman that doesn't feel wanted or loved at all.

Got to be a very weak man to deliver this kind of abuse and pain into a woman's world who wants nothing but the best for you. In Niema's case, she was caught up in a world wind of physical scars and mental anguish that she covered up very well when she was around her friends and family. Niema cried as she looked at her face in the bathroom mirror. The intensity of her pain was at an extremely high level.

She was filled with rage but couldn't bring herself to hurt the man that she loved. She wanted to tell her brother about the abuse, but she couldn't find the words to come out of her mouth. She felt trapped and alone when she was with Nitty. It didn't feel like home at all when they were together it felt like a prison. "Hey Niema." Come in here and try on these new kicks I brought you." Nitty sat in the living room with two boxes of air max.

Lime green and grey joints with the black trim. He tried his sneakers on while he waited for his girl to come out of the bathroom. "What the fuck you are doing in there?" I want you to see what I brought for you. Nitty had a very short temper but he tried to keep his cool because he felt fucked up about what he'd just done.

Niema wiped her tears with a wash cloth that she ran under warm water. She patted her eye that was black and blue very softly and then dried her face with a towel. Opening the bathroom door, she was a nervous wreck and didn't know what to expect from Nitty once she came out. She finally walked into the living room and sat down at the edge of the couch. "Look what I bought you baby. I'm sorry. Damn I love you so much.

Look at this shit. I'm so sorry baby. "Nitty repeated himself as he looked at Niema's face. He hugged her and promised her that he would never hit her again. He gave her the box and she tried on her new kicks and forgave her man for treating her like a punching bag.

Nitty pulled out a credit card machine and started running numbers from active debit and credit cards. Niema was learning how to pull scams though Nitty and he had her running social security numbers at her job every time a client came in for an appointment. Nitty was ready to teach her some new tricks on how to steal the numbers off debit and credit cards straight from the machine. Niema had a list of chicks who were ready to go to the mall to boost or use a stolen credit card to buy an enormous amount of clothing. Then go back to the mall to either return the clothing for its original price or sell it to make a profit on the streets.

Credit card fraud and scams was a money maker just like any other illegal activity if you were good at what you do and had enough balls to do it money was at your beck and call.

At any given moment; don't get caught. Niema did every and anything she could possibly do to keep her man. She was willing to do damn near anything for the dick. She put Kizz on to the fraud and they both started running cards together. The phone rang three times before Niema could answer. The missed call went straight to her voice mail as she gave her man her undivided attention. "What the fuck is this bitch doing?" Kizz hung up and put her phone in her pocket as the visitors jumped off the bus and walked into the building.

Looking at the line, she saw Mona standing there waiting patiently to be called on a visit. Kizz winked at Mona and proceeded to take the ID's and assist each visitor before the inmates arrived on a visit. What up Boo?" Mona smiled as she approached Kizz on the line.

"Mona put your belongings inside of one of the lockers and have a seat until the inmate is called on a visit. Kizz mentioned. Looking at Mona with a stern look on her face. Each visitor was patted down and checked before they sat inside of the visiting room. As Mona stepped inside, she started smiling as soon as she saw Vince. "Mona. My baby. How are you? Vince greeted Mona with a big hug and a kiss.

"I miss you so much Vince. We all do. So glad that they moved you closer to us so that we can come see you more often. Tony is out Vince. I can't believe it he surprised me, and the girls and we haven't left each other's site." Vince just smiled as he looked into Mona's eyes. "I heard he got out, he wrote me and gave me his new number. I'm glad Tony touched down and he's back on the streets.

I spoke to him this morning. He gave me some great feedback on his new connects. You all mean the world to me you hear. You make sure to keep a tight circle and take care of one another no matter what." Vince whispered. Looking around at the Correctional Officers in the room. "I love you Mona and I'm happy that you grew up to be a strong responsible young lady. Stay smart and keep writing those stories.

Send everyone my love and give all the girls and Tony a big hug for me." The visit was coming to an end as the CO's made their announcement. Vince and Mona got up and gave each other a big hug. As she hugged Vince, she passed him a balloon filled with small bundles of cocaine. Vince quickly took the balloon and held it tightly in his hand.

Mona hugged Vince a little tighter and told him how much she loved him. As Vince walked out of the room, Mona just cried and waved him off as he went back to his cell. The visit was over, and Mona left the jail in one piece. She was shitting bricks sitting on that visit with those drugs on her. She couldn't believe that she was able to make it happen. She thought about Kizz and couldn't wait to call her.

Then she realized that her phone was dead and couldn't call anyone even if she wanted to. On her way home, she stopped on the avenue to pick up a fresh pair of sneakers and then headed over to Niema's crib. "Niema. Mona yelled. Knock... knock... knock." Niema, open the door. Mona knocked on Niema's door several times waiting for her to let her into the apartment.

"Who the fuck is that banging on the door? Nitty shouted. Looking at the door with his eyes wide open. Knock… knock… knock." Mona continued to knock at the door. "I know you in there bitch, I saw your car sitting outside let me in. Niema ran to the bathroom to look at her face and proceeded to put a little make up on her eye to cover the bruise. While Niema was inside of the bathroom, Nitty went to the door to look through the peephole.

"Oh, it's Mona." Nitty smirked. Opening the door to let Mona inside. "It took you long enough damn. If I had somebody chasing me I would be fucked up right now." Mona shouted. Pushing her way through the door. "I'm tired as hell. Just came back from seeing Vince. That visit had me shook. Where the hell is Niema?"

Mona looked around the apartment waiting for her friend to come out of the bathroom. As she sat her sneakers down on the couch, she noticed the two pair of kicks on the floor. Oh shit, I just brought the same thing. Mona smiled while she pulled out her fresh new air max in the same exact color as Niema and Nitty. "Yeah them joints is fire. Just picked us up a pair today."

Nitty looked at the sneakers Mona was trying on and smiled. Niema finally walked out of the bathroom looking nervous as hell. "Hey Mona. What you doing here so early? Niema asked. Walking into the kitchen to poor her a shot of vodka. "Early! Bitch it's one o'clock. Let me tell you what happened today.

I couldn't wait to get over here and tell you about the visit with Vince. Mona mentioned. Excited about seeing Vince. Vince looks really good. He told me to tell everyone hello and he sends his love to you. He told me everything he's been doing on the inside and he was in very good spirits. I went up there to bring him some coke. Girl I was fucking scared as hell on that visit with those drugs on me.

I saw Kizz on the visit and she had everything set up for me to do my thing. It felt like a fucking movie scene giving Vince that balloon. He took that shit and kept it moving." Mona laughed. Looking at Niema happy to be sitting on her couch and not in a jail cell. "You are crazy. Niema laughed. I'm glad you got out of there Mona and I'm happy that Vince is okay.

So glad that he is closer now so that we are able to go and see him on the regular." Nitty went into the bedroom so that Niema and Mona could talk. "I see you went and copped the lime green joints Mona them shits is hot. I'm trying to find something nice and tight to go with those. Niema chuckled. Sipping on her shot of vodka. Mona noticed that Niema was a little distant and she was trying to feel her vibe and figure out why.

She saw that Niema kept pulling her hair close to her face covering up her eye. Then Niema went into the kitchen to put her shades on. "Why you wearing shades in the crib? Ain't no sun in here. Mona just stared at Niema with a funny look on her face. Niema didn't answer her as she began to iron her jeans.

Mona walked up to her friend and pulled off her shades. She was shocked to see the black eye under the makeup. "Oh, my goodness. Did he do this to you? Mona whispered. "This mother fucker up in here kicking your ass and you acting like everything is okay. Oh hell no. He about to get fucked up." Mona was in shock looking at Niema's face. "Please don't tell Tony Mona. It was a mistake.

We had a fight and he just hit me too hard that's all. Please don't tell my brother about this I am begging you. Nitty loves me and I love him. I promise, you will never see no shit like this ever again." Niema pleaded with Mona not to tell anyone about her black eye especially Tony. She knew if Tony found out about this he would kill Nitty immediately.

Niema was shitting bricks because she knew damn well that Mona was telling Tony soon as she left her house. "Ok Niema, I won't say anything. If this mother fucker put his hands on you again, I swear to god he is dead. Mona whispered into her friend's ear reassuring her that she will keep her secret if it never happened again. Mona hugged her friend as she started to cry. Niema was frightened as she confided in Mona to keep her secret of abuse.

She didn't want to lose the only man she had. She'd rather continue to get disrespected and punched in the face than to lose the love of her life. The sad reality of a woman who loves a man who treats her like shit. She's been enduring the abuse for so long that she just learned to deal with it and make it apart of her daily routine like everything was cool.

Niema's been living in agony for years until Mona walked into her apartment and saw her pain. "Ok Niema, I won't tell anyone about this I promise. Mona hugged Niema looking into the air thinking of ways she wanted to see Nitty dead. She was pissed off and furious that he was in the same apartment sitting up with her friend beating her ass every time he was good and ready. *"This nigga is a fucking coward."*

Mona thought to herself. She was disgusted as she continued to hug her crying friend. Mona kissed Niema as they both made their way into her kitchen. Mona went into the fridge to grab some orange juice, so she could make herself a drink. Everything will work out just fine Niema. It always does. Mona poured her a glass of orange juice with a shot of vodka.

She lied through her teeth when she told Niema that she would keep her secret. Mona was pissed off and she couldn't wait to get out of Niema's house, so she could call Tony and the rest of the girls to tell them what Nitty did to her face. *"I be dammed if I let this bitch ass mother fucker get away with harming one of my closest friends."* Mona thought to herself as she picked up her sneakers and placed them back inside of the box. Mona kissed Niema before she left her apartment and told her she would contact the chicks who wanted to go to the mall with her later that evening.

Walking out the door, Mona had Tony's number on speed dial. She looked at her phone eager to dial his number. Pressing the elevator, she couldn't believe that Niema was in an abusive relationship.

She wanted to tell Tony so bad, but also wanted to keep her word with Niema. Stepping into the elevator, Mona looked up and saw Beno standing inside. "What's up Mona? Beno asked. Holding the elevator door open. "Hey Beno. Mona replied. Staring at her phone trying not to make eye contact. "Yo! Where the hell is Kema? I need to speak with her. I knocked on her door but there was no answer and she hasn't been answering her phone calls for a few days. Is everything alright?

My brother Dirk's been missing in action also. Beno looked very concerned when he asked about Kema. "Oh, Kema went to Florida for the weekend to attend her sister's wedding. She didn't call you? I would have let you know Beno, my bad I thought you already spoken to her.

Mona was lying through her teeth looking at Beno with a straight face. "Oh ok. I left a package at her crib that I wanted to pick up. Just let her know Ima need that when she gets back. Listen, when you see Tony, have him give me a call I need to holler at him about something. Matter of fact, if you see my brother have him call me as well. Beno gave Mona a hug and walked out of the elevator.

Mona shook her head up and down agreeing with Beno and then watched him walk out of the building. She was shaking like a leaf seeing flash backs of Dirk's body dead in Kema's apartment. When Mona came back to her senses, she forgot all about Niema getting her ass kicked and went straight to the liquor store to get herself a stiff drink.

CHAPTER 7

PRINCESS

You girls have ten minutes to get dressed. The next act will be finished in fifteen. Why are you girls sitting there like you don't have to be on the stage in a few minutes. There will be no cocaine before showtime." Princess shouted. Walking into the dressing room pointing at the lines of coke on the table. "Come over here Victoria let me zip you up. You all look beautiful let's work ladies, shake a tail feather chop-chop." Princess stormed around the club making sure all her girls were at their best.

She had a show tonight and some of the richest millionaire investors and entrepreneurs would be inside of her establishment looking for beautiful woman to spend their money on. Everything needed to be perfect. From the seating area, to the food, to the music and the dancers attire. Princess wanted everything to look elegant. 'Make It Rain' is a beautiful gentlemen's club out in Long Island ran and owned by Princess Estevan.

The club was enormous and had a big showroom and stage where the dancers performed and teased their customers. Her dancers dressed very elegantly and looked like money. Princess played no games when it came to her customers. She catered to all their needs and left them begging for more.

Her girls would do exotic performances ripping each piece of clothing off with a strip tease from out of this world. All her dancers were beautiful in every flavor. There were Black, White, Cuban Italian and Puerto Rican women with big boobs and tight asses ready to make a fortune.

Princess had the best clientele list. Her customers were all rich and very successful. They were very generous and expected nothing but the best. Plenty customers on her clientele list were mob bosses like her father Frederico Estavan who's nick named Rico, were all tied into many entities of the drug game. Princess grew up in Long Island around a slew of mob bosses.

As a young girl, she and her little brother learned the lifestyle very quickly and had to take on various rolls in the drug trafficking business while her father called all the shots. Rico's lifestyle placed his family in the very best houses, cars, and schools. She learned everything from her pops. She was a lady of steel with whips and high heels. She learned how to shoot and carried a pistol at thirteen years old. Her upbringing was different than the average teen age girl. Her Father Italian and mother black, she grew up very rough around the edges with her fingers on the trigger. At family gatherings, her grandmother would make her chop up onions garlic and tomatoes stirring the pasta sauce for the sausages and meatballs in the kitchen while her mother and father bagged up kilos of cocaine with an enormous amount of money all over a big pool table down in the basement of their home.

She had to be tough and was raised to shoot and kill because her family was always a target. When her father went to prison for killing the man who murdered her mother, he pleaded self-defense and ended up serving five years in prison with the help of a judge that he knew for many years who took his case and got his sentence reduced.

Princess and her brother took over their father's business with the help of her uncles and opened several clubs and warehouses distributing drugs and kept everything running until their father returned home.

Drug deals were constant at the club and everyone who had big pockets; came to the club to party and spend large amounts of money for cocaine and pussy.

"Well, hello. Welcome to 'Make It Rain gentleman. Here are two bottles of Moet complementary from Princess. Would you like to place an order from the menu?" The waitress who walked over to the table was wearing an exotic cocktail dress that stopped at the tip of her ass. Her dress barely covered the nipples of her breasts as she leaned over to show the customer the specials for the day.

"We got lobster tails, sautéed and fried shrimps with your choice of pasta or rice. We also have fish and chips and buffalo wings on the menu for the night. The waitress licked her lips as she eased up from the table fixing her dress. "Damn! Do you come with that order? I'll have two orders of lobster tails and sautéed shrimps.

Shit!" Tony's eyes were wide open as he stared at the waitress tucking her breasts back into place. Clay laughed. Watching Tony make his moves on the waitress. "No sweetheart. I don't come with your order, but we have several ladies here who would love to show you a hell of a time. I'll be back gentlemen; your order will be ready for you shortly. Tony and Clay watched the waitress ass as she walked away.

"This joint is on fire. I'm loving this Clay. How the fuck are we supposed to conduct business with all this pussy around?" Tony asked. Staring at all the dancers on stage. "This is what we do Tony chill out and enjoy the show. We are going to be here a lot. You'll get used to it after a while trust me."

Clay reassured Tony that he would be around the gentlemen's club quite often. There's was a live jazz band playing music setting the tone in the room as Princess made her entrance. She was dressed beautifully in a long gown sequence and rhinestones hugging her boobs. "Hello gentlemen. I am so glad you could make it tonight, we have a fabulous showroom full of beautiful women who are here to cater to all your needs.

Are you enjoying your champagne? Princess asked. Sitting down across from Tony and Clay. The two gentlemen were amazed by her beauty and took a minute to reply. "Uhh! Yes, Yes. It's delicious, thanks for having us. Tony replied. Staring at Princess from across the table. "Oh, It's my pleasure. Any friend of my father's is a friend of mines."

Princess smiled. Staring back at Tony with her hazel eyes. Tony was amazed by her beauty. "I hear you just got out of the pen, welcome home. I'm sure you can use some real satisfaction tonight. I hope you can stick around for a while. Whatever you fellas need, feel free to ask we have it all. Drinks, coke, food, pussy, you name it we got it all. My father just arrived, I will let him know that you are here. Princess got up from the table and walked away.

"Oh my god! She is fucking gorgeous. Clay! You saw that shit? Tony asked. Gulping his Moet. "She was staring directly at me. This chick is serious. Clay laughed. "She wasn't looking at you, she was staring at me mother fucker now, have a seat. Tony chuckled. Pouring himself and Clay another glass of Moet.

Frederico Estevan entered the club wearing a tan business suit very dapper and sharp. He is greeted by his daughter with a hug and kiss on the cheek. Princess discussed some business at a table by the kitchen with her father before pointing into Tony and Clay's direction. Rico looked over and is intrigued to see the two-gentleman awaiting his presence. "Gentlemen. Welcome to the gentlemen's club. I hope our ladies are treating you well.

What a great night to make some money. Rico chuckled. Rubbing his hands together. I'm Rico and I'm sure you already met my beautiful daughter Princess. Rico stated. Reaching across the table, shaking Tony's hand. "Yes, I have and it's a pleasure to meet the both of you. Tony replied. Looking Rico straight in the eyes.

Both Rico and Princess sat at the table to discuss business. It's a great feeling to be out the pen isn't it. Rico mentioned. Pouring himself a glass of Moet. "Let's focus on doing things right. We run a very lucrative business and that busy is distributing pure cocaine. There are many safe houses and networks that move kilos of cocaine from their businesses. The purest cocaine comes from Cuba, in which is sent down to Miami and then to NYC.

The cartel moves these drugs through various businesses such as this one. Many people are paid a great salary to travel and test these drugs as well as traffic from state to state. This is where you come to mind my friend. I have done plenty drug deals with both of your uncles Vince and Sammy god rest his soul.

Doing business with those gentlemen was incredible. There were never any problems between the two. We all may have witnessed numerous murders from bodies of people who have stolen from our safe houses and made an example of by shooting off their hands or killing them in front of a family members. There were plenty great memories of us as well coming up hustling in South Side Jamaica Queens. We made millions together and we spent a lot of that money with the community.

People never talk about the good shit drug dealers do. They will always remember the bad. In most cases, you just got to live and let live. Fuck what people think and continue to make this fucking money.

The difference between a crackhead and a drug dealer is that the crackhead will do anything to get the drug, and the drug dealer will sell to anyone to make that paper stack. No one is ever forced to used drugs. Drugs are distributed in the finest businesses. Pharmacies get away with killing citizens every single day, but the law wants to put people like us under the jail and throw away the key. Anything that I do I do it from the heart. I take my business very seriously. If you are loyal to me I will treat you like royalty.

If the tables turn and I find out that you are a rat or a snake, I will kill you. Shit like this becomes very sad for me because I never want to cut the throat of someone who works with me. What I admire, and love is pure loyalty.

Without trust you are a dead man walking. When I put my product into your hands, I expect you to treat that product like your life is depending on it. I ask that every ounce of cocaine that I put into your hands, reaches its destination. Every dollar of money counted and placed into suitcases, will be sent to me, every penny. If you can do that my friend, then you will live a great wealthy life. If you cross me, your life will end. The distribution is simple.

Stay low key and move the product from one point to the other." As Rico explained the rules of his business, he quickly snapped his fingers for one of his men to hand him two brief cases. He then sat the brief cases on the table and turned the brief cases towards Tony and Clay and signaled them both to open each one.

The two fellas looked at one another and opened the brief cases to see forty kilos of cocaine sitting inside. There were twenty kilos in each case. "You want to make real money? Well here we are. Working for me will be a great experience don't fuck it up. Rico chuckled. Staring at Tony and Clay with a devilish grin. I have one job for you to do before you go. Rico mentioned. Looking at his watch for the time. There is a man in this club that I need robbed.

He has many diamonds at his home inside of a safe behind the picture of George Washington in his office. I know because I was there yesterday at his place having lunch with him sharing details of a real estate venture. He is very wealthy and will spend a ton of money on my girls tonight.

The diamonds inside of his safe belong to me. They were stolen from my home after my wife was shot in the head and killed. Before I killed the man, who killed my wife, he sold the diamonds to the gentleman at table number six. I was able to find the bastard who killed the love of my life through a family friend who owns a bar out in Long Island where he sat and bragged about robbing my house for the diamonds over drinks. His face was captured on the cameras at my home and was marked the day he killed the mother of my children.

He was shocked to see me walk into the bar that night. We tortured him for many days ripping him to pieces limb by limb trying to get him to tell us where the diamonds were before I shot him in the head and he gave us nothing.

It's ironic how the shit you go through serves a purpose in the end. The partner of the mother fucker who killed my wife, served time with me in prison. He came clean about everything that he did and told me everything that happened the day they robbed my house for drugs and money. I assured him I wouldn't kill him if he shared every detail of the robbery.

After feeding him a pack of cigarettes and a week of commissary money; he sang like a canary and told me who his partner sold the diamonds to and then I slit his throat in the shower and sent him off to hell where he belongs. Losing the mother of my children was the hardest thing to bear with two young teenagers who had to take over my business. I'm very blessed to be out of the pen and I will never go back."

Rico explained the horrible events of his wife's murder and how he came to find out about his diamonds that were stolen from him. "Damn, that was fucking deep. I would love to get your diamonds and anything else that belongs to you. Where does this mother fucker live? Does he have any relatives? We need to know every detail about him before we make our move. Tony stated. Eyes wide open giving Rico his undivided attention.

"He lives alone in Massapequa New York, Nassau County. He has a mini mansion, owns two dogs and has an alarm system. There is a key sitting under a big plant that sits right in front of his house. You are going to find it and get into the house. If the alarm system goes off, don't panic. Press these four numbers and the alarm will stop ringing.

This job is very simple. I will keep him here entertained for the night until your task is finished. Once you get back to the club with my diamonds, you are free to enjoy the rest of the night and I will give you the kilos of coke at the site of your return. Everything was set. Rico shook hands with his men and watched them both exit the club. Rico was excited to bring Tony on board with his entourage. He felt very good to be working with the nephews of his longtime friends whom he'd done business with for over two decades.

Rico went to talk business with the gentleman over at table number six. "Hello Mr. Roberts. Nice to have you here at the club tonight. Before you continue enjoying yourself with our beautiful ladies at your beck and call; I'd like to seal the deal on the business venture we started at your home.

Rico sat down at Mr. Roberts table and pulled out his book receipts and a big bag of money. "I am delighted to do business with you Rico we have your money ready and cleaned for you at our bank and have everything legal and legit. All checking accounts and safe deposits are placed into your daughter Princess name. We cleaned the money through her beauty salons and restaurant. Here are your bank statements and temporary cards. You will be able to make withdrawals and deposits at the bank as soon as tomorrow.

There will be an official master card mailed to your home in seven business days. When you go to the bank, you never ask for me or have any contact with me personally. You can go in like a regular banker and conduct business like a regular customer.

This money that I am laundering will never be traced back to me; it will be as if you opened an account with an agent who secured all your banking needs. I appreciate your business Mr. Estevan and I am glad to be of help to you. Mr. Roberts shook Rico's hand and thanked him for banking with him at his branch not knowing that it would be the last hand that he would ever shake. "Yes, well of course, it's a pleasure doing business with you also. Please enjoy yourself I will put these up in a safe place.

Princess make sure Mr. Robert gets the very best. Place him in one of the VIP rooms and have Sylvia give him a fantastic blow job. I'll be back shortly. Rico went to put his paperwork and bank cards into his glove compartment.

Princess listened to her father's orders and escorted the gentleman to the VIP section of the club. Tony arrived at the house in Massapequa. He parked and waited for Clay to pull up. Few minutes later he saw Clay pulling up right in front of him. "I think this is the house right here. Tony whispered. Looking at the address on the paper. "Yeah! This is it. Pop the trunk. Clay replied. "We need to get in, get the diamonds and get out." Tony walked up the stairs and looked for the plant in front of the house.

"Bullseye! There's the key open up the door." Tony passed the key to Clay after scooping it from under the plant. Walking into the house, all the lights were off, so Tony used the light from his cell phone. Why the hell are you using your cell phone when we can use this?

Clay asked. Turning on the flashlight. Both men entered the office. Looking around they saw that the office was gigantic. Ok! We are looking for the George Washington painting Tony. You go to that side and I'll check over here." Tony looked up as Clay directed him to the other side of the office. "The painting is right over your head." Tony chuckled. As they both looked at the painting sitting right over Clay's head. "Look around to make sure no one else is in here while I buss this safe."

While Tony went to the other side of the office, Clay began to check the numbers to the combination. "Don't move mother fucker. I'll put a bullet in you so quick you won't know what hit you." The old lady screamed with a shotgun aimed directly at Clay.

"Ok! You got it. Clay turned around with his hands in the air. "Get on your knees now mother fucker." The old lady screamed to the top of her lungs cocking the shot gun she was holding in her hands. "Listen it's not what it looks like. I'm here to deliver something from Dr. Weebler. Clay mentioned. Lying his ass off. "Who the fuck is Dr. Weebler mother fucker? I don't know no Dr. Weebler. Don't play me for no fool I know you are here to rob my husband blind.

I'm not stupid I can see the safe open. As the old lady continued screaming with her shotgun pointed at Clay's head; Tony ran up on her and hit her in the head with a statue. The blow from the statue hit her so hard that it killed her instantly. The old lady fell, dropping the shotgun onto the floor. "It took you long enough. Where the fuck were you?

Clay asked. Sweating bullets. I went to the other side of the office like you told me too. I didn't know this old bitch was going to come in here ready to shoot the shit out of you. Rico said no one else lived here. Fuck all that; look I found the diamonds. They were inside of his desk. Tony mentioned. Showing Clay, a pouch full of diamonds. Clay looked at the diamonds with his eyes wide open then looked inside of the safe. "Oh shit. Lucky, you went to the other side of the room.

There were no diamonds inside of the safe, but stacks of money stared right at them. Tony and Clay filled a bag full of money and left the house. "Damn! Why did that old lady have to come down stairs? This definitely wasn't part of the plan."

Clay snarled. Looking up at the house separating the money in his car. "I know, she came down and got dealt with let's get the fuck up out of here." Tony took his share of the money, ran to his car, and they both pulled off in their rides and headed back to the strip club. "Gentlemen. You both got back so soon. I hope you have good news for me." Rico grinned. Walking toward Tony and Clay. Sitting down, Rico waited for Tony to answer him with a serious look on his face. "Yes, we found exactly what you were looking for."

Tony pulled the diamonds out of his pocket and handed them over to Rico. "AHHH... My diamonds. This is an enlightening moment my friend. What you two did just now shows me how much I can trust you both. You made me a very happy man tonight.

We must celebrate." Rico clapped his hands and asked the waitress to bring over the finest Cognac. "There was a slight problem at the house. There was an old lady inside and she pulled out a shotgun on Clay. I had to hit her in the head and I think I may have killed her. We didn't check to see if she was dead, we just got out of there as quickly as we could." Tony mentioned. "Is that so. Well the good thing is that you both got out of there without anyone seeing you.

If she threatened your life what else were you to do. You went in there to get back what's rightfully mines. She should have stayed out of it and maybe she would be sipping on some tea instead of passed out or dead. I asked you to bring me the diamonds, anything extra you may have found is yours.

I am fully aware that Mr. Roberts keeps a load of money in his safe as well. Did you find any money?" Rico asked. Tony shook his head up and down. "The money is yours." Rico got up and signaled the fellas to come with him as he walked over to the VIP section. Mr. Roberts was enjoying himself tremendously as he received a blowjob from a big tit stripper at the club. Rico snapped his fingers and signaled the stripper to leave out of the room. Soon as the stripper left, Rico took out his gun walking up to Mr. Roberts and put a bullet in his chest.

Mr. Roberts held his chest pleading for his life. Rico then shot him in the head and pushed his body onto the plastic that was already on the floor. Tony and Clay were shocked staring at the man as they helped Rico roll him up.

Two large men came into the room picking up the plastic with Mr. Roberts inside of it. They took him out back into an alley and placed him inside of a caravan. Rico followed the men and ordered them to go to Mr. Roberts house to pick up the old lady that Tony hit over the head. "Looks like you can use some sexual healing. Princess whispered into Tony's ears, while walking away from him slowly.

Tony stared at Princess ass enjoying the view. When Rico returned, he sat down at a table with Tony and Clay and made good on his words. Here is your brief case Mr. Tony and Mr. Clay. I am giving you both a large amount of cocaine and I expect fifty percent back. You both have shown me a great amount of trust and I am most certainly pleased with your performance tonight.

These diamonds are worth millions and it is a pleasure to have them back in my possession once again. Take this coke and stash it in a very safe place. We will discuss business later. Right now, let's enjoy the view and drink up. Rico shook the hands of both gentlemen and took a drink with them to celebrate their new journey. Tony grinned toasted with his new-found partners in crime as Princess stared at him with lust in her eyes. It's ironic how so much pain can lead to so much pleasure. In this line of business, you just never know what to expect.

CHAPTER 8

The Clique

'Ring… Ring. The phone rang a dozen times with no answer. Beno was furious and wanted answers. He wanted to know where his stash was, why Kema bailed on him, and find out what happened to his brother. "Kema, when you get this message give me a call asap. Where the fuck are you bitch? I want my stash that I left up in your crib and my money." Listening to Beno's messages aggravated the hell out of Kema. She hated picking up the phone with him on the other end asking her a million questions.

"I swear I want him dead, I can't take this shit no more. Kema shouted. Throwing her phone onto Mona's sofa. "Sometimes you get what you ask for and that just might be a great idea. Mona replied. The phone rang again with Beno's name on it. 'Knock… knock… knock. The banging on the door startled everyone inside of Mona's apartment. "Who is it? Mona screamed. Running to the door.

"It's Tony, let me in. Looking through the peephole, Mona saw Tony standing in front of her door holding onto a black brief case. "Tony what are you doing here? I thought you were going away for a few days? Mona asked. Eager to see what Tony had to say. "Slight change of plans Mona. Tony answered. Walking into the apartment placing the briefcase on the table.

"What's in the briefcase Tony? Is everything okay? Mona walked over to the table and sat down. "Everything's great. We got a shit load of money and coke and I can just kiss your pretty face right now." Tony kissed Mona on her lips and opened the briefcase. Kai, Niema, Kizz and Kema got up from the couch in the living room and walked towards the table in the dining room. "Holy shit! Where the fuck did you get that? Niema asked.

Staring at all the kilos of cocaine on the table. "That's an awful lot of cocaine Tony. Who the fuck is supposed to bag this shit up? Kizz shouted. "First of all, lower your voice. You know how thin these fucking walls are damn. Sometimes I think I'm dealing with a bunch of idiots."

Tony shouted. Taking one of the kilos out of the brief case slitting it open with a knife. "No, he didn't just call us some idiots after all the shit we do for him." Niema whispered. Rolling her eyes. "Listen this shit is going take some time. I hope you don't expect to have all of this coke bagged up this weekend." Mona whispered. Staring at the briefcase. "No! We are going to keep it like it is, the way it's always been and have two kilos ready every Thursday night. Ain't shit change but the weather.

We are back in full effect. This dude Rico is a heavy hitter. I really respect this guy. He trusts me, and I won't let him down. Reminds me so much of Vince word. We went out to his daughter's strip club and popped a few bottles the shit was crazy.

I had a fucking ball. Tony chuckled. Opening a big bottle of Hennessy. Strip club, I bet you had a good time. Mona replied. Puffing on the blunt that Niema passed her. "Mona shut up. Let's worry about all this paper we about to make." Tony pulled out a stack of money and paid each girl three thousand dollars apiece to get four kilos of coke bagged up by Thursday. The girls gladly accepted his offer and began bagging up immediately. It felt like old times again. The Clique were all under the same roof.

The love was in the air and the smiles were genuine and real. "All the days I prayed in that jail cell has led me up to this moment right now. I'm in my element I'm happy I'm with my family. You can't get no better than this shit here. If we focus and move right, we all are going to be straight.

This new connect right here is where it's at. My main man Vince told me Rico was a good dude. I'm glad I followed through on his word." Tony was feeling good and wanted to stay that way. "I'm just happy to see your smiling face again Bro. Whoever this Rico cat is, kudos to him for putting you back on top. They don't make men like him no more." Niema mentioned. "He is definitely a rare jewel.

So cool to see my family back together under one roof. Mona smiled. While the girls sat at the table bagging up a pile of cocaine, Kema's phone rang again. "Ahh, Shit! I'm sick and tired of this mother fucker calling me. He's been calling all fucking night. "Kema looked at her phone as it went to voicemail. "Tony, we got to do something about Beno.

He is not going to stop until he talks to one of us about his stash and money that was left at Kema's crib. I had bumped into him one day when I came from Niema's house after she got beat up by Nitty. He had me shook in the elevator. I thought Beno knew about his brother and Devita and was coming to hurt one of us out of revenge of his brother getting killed.

When he just asked if I saw Kema and left after giving me a hug; I almost fainted in that fucking hallway. "Mona was shaking thinking about how scared she was when she saw Beno. "Wait! What happened with Niema and Nitty? This dude beating your ass now. When the fuck was you going to tell me that?

Or you just like for mother fuckers to whip on your ass.
"Tony was disgusted when he heard about Niema's boyfriend beating her up. "You know damn well I'm not going to sit around and let anybody put their hands and feet on any one of you. Anybody that puts their hands on a woman is a fucking coward and a sucker. Only a bitch ass nigga will do some shit like that. I bet his pussy ass wouldn't come at me like that, but he wanna beat the shit out of you and you just sitting there condoning that shit.

You not no broke bitch! Why you allow him to put his hands on you Niema? I'm so pissed off I can't even think about this shit right now. What I do know, is if he put his hands on you again; he's fucking dead."

Tony just put the word out that he would kill Nitty if he laid another hand on his sister. Niema sat at the table rolling her eyes staring at Mona with a screw face. Mona didn't look at Niema at all. She concentrated on placing the cocaine into a small baggie bopping her head to the music playing on the radio. "You didn't have to blurt my business out like that Mona; I thought I could trust you.

I should have never confided in you bitch. Niema whispered. "Confided in me, the same chick that held on to your fucking secret for two months. Bitch please. You probably been getting beat since you met the mother fucker, don't put this shit on me. I'm tired of holding on to your secrets. That nigga needs to get checked anyway fuck that.

Mona got up and walked out of the dining room. Kema grabbed a card and start sniffing lines of coke in front of everybody. "Got damn bitch, slow the fuck down. If you want some all you gotta do is let me know." Tony took a big pile of cocaine and gave some to Kema for personal use. "Listen, don't be using my shit. We gotta make money off this shit. You make enough money to buy your own shit. Let me find out you are stealing my shit without me knowing and Ima get one of the girls to fuck you up."

Tony made it very clear of what would happen to Kema if she took his shit. Kema agreed, took a quick bump, then put her stash he gave her into her pocket. We ride or die. I need to be able to trust every one of you. If there's no trust, there's nothing. Either get with the program or get left.

Tony started weighing all the coke and separating the bags. The mood in the apartment was a little tense, but nothing they haven't all seen before. Tony was feeling good and didn't give a fuck about anything but chasing that paper. He had a new connect and was back on top like he planned. He was feeling himself once again. His connect was on fire and it spread wide from Spanish Harlem to ATL. The Clique hustled and bagged up Tony's work ready to set it off on anyone who moved funny.

They were making tons of money and had a shit load of cocaine. Rico called up Tony to put him on to a big deal coming up from someone who wanted to buy an enormous amount of cocaine. Meanwhile, there was a problem that none of them saw coming.

Beno was on their tale. Ever since he saw Mona in Baisley projects, he was very suspicious and wanted answers as to why Kema has been missing in action. Especially after she never returned his work and never gave him back his cash. Once his brother Dirk stop returning his phone calls, he knew something was wrong. He called Kema every single day and her phone just went to voicemail. That left him confused and furious at the same time. He started tracking his brother's moves and came up with absolutely nothing.

His alternatives were slim, so he went to the hood one night and just watched Mona's moves. He started following Mona around for a whole week and found out where her new apartment was located.

There he was, parked outside of Mona's crib like a night hawk waiting patiently until she came out, so he could get to the bottom of everything. Beno needed answers about his money, about his stash, and about his brother who's been missing for over a month with no clues as to where to find him. He called the precincts, checked the jails, called the morgues and came up with nothing. He knew for a fact that something happened to Dirk, and he knew one of those bitches who bagged up for him knew exactly where he was.

It was twelve midnight and Beno was still parked outside of Mona's complex. He hadn't seen any movement from her place since he parked there earlier that day.

Suddenly, Mona came out of the building carrying a big duffle bag full of cocaine. She had to make a quick drop and was on her way to make it happen. Beno watched Mona as she walked to her car, opening her trunk to place the duffle bag inside. Closing the trunk, Mona looked around to make sure the coast was clear; then she jumped into her car and started the engine. She pulled off slowly and headed to her destination and Beno slowly followed behind her.

Mona bumped her music as she waited at the light. Her drop was a couple of blocks away and she had a couple of minutes to spare so she decided to stop at the corner to get some jerk chicken from the Jamaican restaurant. Parking the car, Beno made the turn and saw Mona stop by the restaurant.

Getting out of the car, Mona saw a car turn it's lights off, but no one got out of it. She thought for a minute but just kept it moving so she can go order some food. Good evening, welcome to Jamaican Soul may I take your order." The gentleman asked kindly with a smile. "Yes, I would like to get two orders of oxtails with potatoes and white rice. I also want an order of Jerk chicken with peas and rice and plantains. Mona looked at the food with amazement.

She loved oxtails and jerk chicken and couldn't make up her mind on what she wanted. Then she thought about the rest of The Clique and placed three more orders. "Excuse me, let me get two orders of stew chicken and another order of oxtails with the order I just made.

Mona sat down and waited patiently for her food. She sent a text to her sister Kai to let her know that she ordered them some Jamaican food from Jamaican Soul. After about five minutes everything was plated up and ready to go. Mona paid for the food, thanked the gentleman who served her, then exited the restaurant.

Mona walked up the block, signaled the car door to open then placed the food in her back seat. Soon as she closed the back door, Beno rushed up on her from behind with a gun. "Don't move bitch. Where the fuck is my money and my stash? "Beno. What are you doing? I don't have your money I swear. Your money was at Kema's house and her place had gotten robbed. She was scared to call you when she came back from vacation.

I swear Beno, I'm telling you the truth. "Listen, I don't give a fuck about you, Tony or that bitch Kema right now. I want what's mines and I'm gonna get it from you even if I have to kill you for it. I've been watching you for a minute and you seem to be making a whole lot of moves for someone who doesn't have any product." Beno mentioned. Looking around holding a pistol to Mona's head.

"Get in the fucking car now." Beno was desperate and ready to kill for his money. I left thirty-five thousand dollars at Kema's apartment and two kilos of cocaine. What did you bitches do with my money? I'm not gonna sit here with you and play any more games Mona. I want my money and my coke, and I want it now. Mona looked at Beno scared to death. "Alright. Alright.

I can get you your money Beno, let me just call my sister and have her bring the money to this location right now. There's no need to get crazy. I can get you your money. "Beno wasn't trying to hear anything she was saying at this point. He just wanted what he gave them and a little more to even the score. "Open up your trunk bitch. Beno shouted. "You better not do nothing funny either or I will shoot you where you stand."

Mona shook her head up and down and agreed to everything that Beno told her. She got out of the car and opened the trunk. Beno kept his gun down low still facing Mona in plain sight so she could see it. He then looked inside of the trunk and saw the duffle bag that Mona was carrying when she came out of the building.

Beno looked at the bag and opened it up. Inside the duffle bag he saw five kilos of cocaine. "Oh, so you bitches must have given my stash to Tony to make money and new connects. You thought you could get away with taking my shit with no repercussions. Beno took the duffle bag and ordered Mona to get back into the car. Mona cried scared for her life pleading with Beno to take the bag and just let her go. "Beno please, take the bag you can have everything in it just take it and let me go." Beno got back into the car with Mona and told her to drive into the alley of the Jamaican restaurant.

Pulling into the alley, Beno opened the door and hit Mona with the butt of his gun. He hit her two times with the gun knocking her unconscious. Mona hit her head on the steering wheel and the car starting honking.

Beno quickly raised Mona's head and put the driver seat down to make it look like she was taking a nap. He wiped the blood from her head with a napkin and took off with the duffle bag. Mona was left in the alley in her car with the food she ordered from the restaurant. She was robbed of Tony's kilos and knocked out cold. "It's been an hour since Mona left with the package for Rico's customer.

Where the fuck is she?" Tony asked. Grabbing for his phone to call her. Tony dialed Mona's number and didn't get any response. "Mona called me about thirty minutes ago and asked me what I wanted from the Jamaican restaurant on Merrick Blvd. You want to go check it out and she if she's still there? Kai asked. "I don't think she would be there, the food doesn't take that long to order.

Let me try her phone one more time." Tony rang Mona's phone more than five times and it kept going to voicemail. Something is fucking wrong, I can feel it. Tony circled around in the living room holding his hands on his head. "Yo! Something just don't feel right. Let's take a ride up to the restaurant and see if she left her phone there. You know how Mona is with phones.

Tony looked over at Kai as they all agreed with her. He and his girls grabbed their sweaters and headed out of the door. "I swear to god, if something happened to her, Ima kill something. The Clique pulled up to the Jamaican restaurant with Tony looking around the block to see if they saw Mona and didn't see her anywhere.

Parking the car, Kai continued looking around. Stepping out of Tony's ride, Kai saw Mona's cell phone on the sidewalk. Picking up her cell phone, they all looked at one another and knew something wasn't right. Tony took his gun out of the car and proceeded to walk up the block, so he could check inside of the restaurant.

"Hello. I would like to know if you've seen this girl come inside to place an order of food from here. She called me from here about forty minutes ago and I just found her cell phone outside in the street on this block." Tony mentioned. He was anxiously waiting for the man behind the counter to let him know if he saw her or not. "Yes. I saw this young lady, she brought oxtails and jerk chicken pretty girl she left the restaurant a while ago.

I saw her outside talking to heavy set guy after she brought her food." The man behind the register described the guy he saw with Mona right after she left with her food. "Did you see his face? How did he look? Kai asked. "The guy was stocky, and dark skinned he had on a jean jacket and a blue baseball cap; that is all I can remember.

The cook from the restaurant had empty boxes piled up inside of the kitchen and proceeded to carry the boxes out back to the trash, so he could make some space for the next pile of boxes of tomato sauce to unload and place into the cabinets. He stepped out back carrying boxes over to the dumpster. Closing the dumpster, he saw a car parked with the lights on and it looked like someone was inside. Walking over to car, he looked around to make sure no one was behind him.

As soon as he reached the car, he could see Mona sitting in the driver seat laying there with her head bleeding unconscious from the blow of the gun. "Oh my god. "Lonnie. Come around back and see this here you know. I knew something was fishy about this car you know. There's a girl laying in the car bleeding out the head. I'm going to call the ambulance and the police right now.

"The cook explained with an accent. Everyone listened to what the cook said and ran around the back of the restaurant in the alley to see what he was talking about. Tony and the girls saw Mona's car and ran as fast as they could to see who was inside. Reaching the car, they could see that Mona was hurt and bleeding from her head. The door was locked from the inside and they had no way of getting in.

Tony then broke the back window and popped the lock to open the door. "Mona. Mona. Wake up. Mona, wake up baby. Who did this to you? Mona didn't respond. Kai and the rest of the girls started crying because they thought she was dead. Tony continued tapping Mona on her cheek trying to wake her up. Mona finally came to, opening her eyes looking up at Tony and The Clique holding her head. "Don't move Mona, just stay still and tell us what happened.

Who did this to you? Tony asked. Ready to kill something. Mona moaned softly as she tried to talk. Her head was killing her as she tried to tell Tony what happened to her. "Tony, it was Beno. He ran up on me after I picked up the food. He said he's been following me for a minute and followed me to my house.

Tony, Beno took the duffle bag with the cocaine. I never made the drop. Beno robbed me Tony. He took the kilos and hit me in the head with his gun. My head is fucking killing me right now. Mona cried. Explaining how Beno just robbed her and took the cocaine he just got from Rico. "Do you want us to take you to the hospital? Your head is bleeding Mona, I think you need to go see a doctor.

"No fuck the doctor, take me home I want to go home right now. Mona shouted. "Oh, this mother fucker put his gun to your head and hit you with it. That nigga gotta die. This mother fucker took five kilos of my coke. It's on now. He done fucked up now. I'm about to send this nigga off to visit his brother six feet under.

"Tony was furious. He couldn't believe Beno would do some shit like that to Mona. He knew it was definitely a problem on his hands. "Beno took Rico's coke and think he not gonna get checked. Who the fuck this nigga thinks he's fucking with. He approached Mona instead of coming straight to me, that was a bitch ass move.

Tony hugged Mona as tight as he could and took her home. "Beno knows where I live now Tony. We gotta be super careful because this nigga can do anything. He didn't say nothing to me about Dirk, he just kept asking me about the stash he left at Kema's crib. I told him that I didn't have it and he had to wait to get in touch with Kema.

He knew exactly where the duffle bag was and grabbed for it soon as I opened the trunk. That mother fucker been watching me, and I didn't even know it. Mona was pissed off. She was tight that she didn't notice Beno following her and watching her every move this whole time. "That's alright. I got something for his mother fucking ass when I catch that fat fuck Ima blow his head off. I have ten kilos left, so I gotta make some moves.

Gotta get this bread back for Rico. "Tony's mind was spinning in every direction. "*Ima make Beno pay when I catch him. He took Rico's coke. All that money lost in one split second. Mona getting robbed all at the same time. Thank god, he didn't kill my best friend.*" Tony held his hands over his forehead thinking of all the shit that just transpired.

He was literally to the point of no return. He knew exactly what he needed to do the get the cash back that he just lost. He had a plan to get that back asap. Tony was upset about the coke, but happy he didn't find Mona dead in that alley and thanked his lucky stars. Tony and The Clique decided to dip on the low for a minute to clear their heads. Pulling into the Ramada Inn, Tony thought of all the crazy shit that popped off since he been home.

"It's been a crazy two months, I tell you that much. Don't worry about this shit Mona, everything will be okay. I will protect you with my life you hear me. I'm not letting you out of my sight for a minute. All I gotta say about Beno is he is a dead man walking. There's no way in hell that I'm going to sit around and let this mother fucker play me like a sucker."

It didn't take long for someone else to piss Tony off. Beno passed that test with flying colors and just signed his own death certificate…

CHAPTER 9

The Heist

The weather was gorgeous. The wind blew lightly as the palm trees moved with the breeze like an Indian summer. It's been a long time since Tony enjoyed himself and it felt great. The shift in scenery was exactly what everyone needed because the last couple of months have been hella crazy. "Listen Ima need a chick to take a trip out to Miami asap. There's a pusher out in Miami who called me up and told me he needed a kilo of cocaine by this weekend but didn't want to risk the trip. He's willing to pay me the extra cash to get the job done.

I let him know that I would get someone to do it for a nice price. He's offering $60,000 for the kilo so we can get a chick a roundtrip flight, pay her to do the job and give her half going and the other half when she comes back. I'll have some of my goons take the trip out with her to make sure she gets the job done. Let me know asap if you have someone in mind who can make it happen." Tony mentioned. Sitting up at the casino in Las Vegas with Clay and The Clique. "You need to meet the rest of Princess girls over at the strip club.

Not the chick we sat with at the table, I'm talking about these other two chicks, they're sister's and these two bitches be double teaming, stripping and doing crazy sex orgies fucking niggas together. They're drug smugglers also.

One of the sister's name Dynasty', she put a half of kilo up her pussy and got that shit through the airport and on the plane with no fucking problem. The chick is about her paper I'm telling you. She will do that shit for a fair price. If I'm not mistaken, she got about $10,000 easy for the last job she did." Clay replied. Staring at Tony with excitement in his eyes. "Damn. That bitch is gully. You think she really be putting that shit up in her kitty? She must have a big ass pussy. How the fuck can she get a half of kilo into her kitty? Ima half to meet this chick to see how she rock." Tony chuckled. Still thinking of the chick Clay just described to him. While Tony and Clay made their way over to the slot machines, Mona and her girls went over to the bar to get everyone some drinks.

A vacation was definitely needed after the shit Beno pulled off and they all just wanted to relax and have a little fun. No matter how much fun they were having, Tony always had some shit on his mind and wanted to discuss business wherever they went. "Can I have a large Pina Colada with an extra shot of vodka please." Kai shouted. Talking to the bartender across the bar at the casino in Las Vegas.

"Matter of fact, let me get two more Pina Coladas and three strawberry daquiris as well." Kai corrected her order before the waitress walked away. "Oh shit, Kai treating. I'm hanging with you all night." Mona giggled. Smiling at her sister at the bar. The casino slots were filled with a variety of people.

There were a bunch of old white men smoking cigarettes with change cups inside of their cup holders filled with coins. The view was crazy, and it was a beautiful night. There were bright lights everywhere. "Did you just hear Tony and Clay talking about these chicks that be smuggling coke to Florida and Miami?" Mona asked. Curiously interested in their conversation. Kai, Kizz and Niema nodded their heads up and down as Mona continued talking.

"More power to them hoes because I be dammed if I'm putting anything that large up my vagina or ass. These chicks got major balls. Glad he found somebody to do that shit because it wasn't going to be me." Kai laughed at Mona as she rolled her eyes sipping on her drink.

"You know you would stick a whole kilo up your ass for Tony. You do anything for his ass stop fronting." Kizz giggled. Laughing at Mona while they sat at the bar. "Yeah, I would do anything for Tony. But there are some things he will not let me do because he doesn't want to risk anything happening. Smuggling drugs to a different country is some other shit. We do a lot of risky shit though I'm not going to front, I'd be lying if I said otherwise.

These chicks Clay mentioned stick shit up their pussy the size of a tennis ball. What the fuck! That ain't happening on my worst day; especially not on no damn airplane. If you get caught doing some shit like that, that's ten to fifteen years tops. Let them chicks master that airplane shit I will stay my little ass down here on these streets and get in where I fit in."

Mona replied. Clay and Tony walked over to the bar to join in on the conversation. Soon as Mona saw Tony approaching the bar, she quickly changed the subject mentioning how nice the casino was. "Don't change the subject on my behalf. I know y'all weren't sitting over here talking about the casino all this time. Miss me with the bullshit Mona I know you better than that." Tony blurted. Signaling the waitress to come to the end of the bar.

"Yes, bring me another strawberry daquiri please. Tony politely asked tipping the waitress with a fifty-dollar bill. "We were talking about the casino and a few other things. I overheard Clay telling you about the tennis ball pussy bitches and I thought my girls needed to hear what he had to say about them".

Tony bussed out laughing when he heard Mona's response. "Tennis ball pussy bitches. Where do you get your info? "You were both talking about these hoes who be smuggling drugs in their kitty don't lie I hear every fucking thing." Everybody at the bar laughed with each other as Mona described every detail after listening to Tony and Clay's conversation. "Well damn, I know not to say some shit around your ass ever again." Clay chuckled. "Who the fuck is Princess anyway?

Is she someone we will be meeting in the future? I try to mind my business, but when you keep mentioning a chick name and nobody ever saw or heard of her; a sister gets a little curious as to who this person is. Come on Tony, you meet everybody we deal with, what's so special about this chick?"

Mona asked. Looking at Tony and Clay waiting for an answer. Clay just looked the other way and focused on his drink. "Everything we do don't need to be said or known. Some things I do Mona is for your own protection. The less shit you know the better. If any one of us gets caught up, what you think these police is going to do? They will eat you for breakfast trying to get any information out of you.

What you don't know might save your fucking life. Stop worrying so much about the shit I don't say and do and practice on the things I do say and do damn. If I need you to know about something I will tell you. Obviously, I included you in the new connect because we are sitting with one of the mother fuckers right now. Pump your brakes a little and trust everything that I do, I do it for a fucking reason."

Tony's point was made, and the conversation was finished. "Now let's go and have ourselves a ball and think about business tomorrow. The girls sat at the bar and bussed out laughing looking at Mona who sat there with the gas face. "I guess he told you. Finally, somebody is bold enough to put Mona in her place. Thanks Tony I think you are the only one that could." Kai patted Tony on the back as she and her girls headed over to the slot machines.

Tony then sat down next to Clay at the bar and finished the conversation from earlier. "Make sure to set that shit up tonight Clay, I need to know if this chick Dynasty is willing to make that move for me asap. This guy Jimmy from Miami is ready to pay the bread as we speak all I need to do is give him the word and it's a done deal.

Get your girl Princess to holler at me so I can meet her girls soon as we get back to New York." "Ok Tony I got you. Matter fact I can give her a call right now." Soon as Clay pulled his phone out, his phone rang with Rico on the other line. "Oh shit, that's Rico right there. "Hello, my friend you have some money for me give me a number." Rico blurted. Waiting on the other end of the receiver. "Give me a few days Rico and I will have everything for you that's a promise."

Clay replied. Not knowing what to tell Rico. He knew if he let Rico know about the robbery it would definitely be a problem. "Ok my friend I take your word and I will be waiting to see you both soon as you get back from Las Vegas. I expect to see a bag full of money at my office once you return."

Rico informed Clay that he wanted to see him and Tony and his money soon as they came back from their vacation. "Ok Rico, I got you. I will hit you up as soon as we get back." Hanging up the phone, Clay was shitting bricks telling Tony what Rico just said. "Rico, wants his money from them kilos he gave us. I didn't know what to say when he asked, I just told him to give us a few days.

He expects to see us as soon as we get back to New York. Listen Tony, if you want I can give you the five kilos Beno took from my stash to get shit right with Rico. I told him to give us a few days, so we should head back to New York as soon as we can to make it happen with these stripper chicks and get this paper up for Rico."

Clay mentioned. "Do you think we should just tell him and get this shit out in the open. I'm good with getting Rico his money but I'm not gonna sit here and feel funny about some shit that I didn't even do. When we make it back to Queens I'll let Rico know myself what really went down." Tony whispered. Sitting at the bar. There was a strip tease show going on at the next club across from the casino.

Tony and Clay headed over to see some tits and ass. As they reached the other side of the street Niema was already over there standing up against the club holding her face. "What the fuck happened to you?" Tony asked. Looking around while holding onto Niema's hands. "Tony let go of me. I have to find Nitty.

He is out here with another bitch I just saw him fucking her inside of the bathroom." Niema tried her best to get away from Tony, but Tony had a firm grip on her wrist. Well if he here with another bitch, why the fuck is your face bleeding?

You got this nigga cheating and beating on you and you sitting out here crying. Where the fuck is this mother fucker at?" Tony couldn't even question his confusion. He just wanted to find Nitty and get to the bottom of the bullshit. "Tony, I don't know. He's inside of the club. Mona, Kizz and Kai are inside as well. I just can't take this shit no more, I can't fuck with him anymore." Niema just cried outside of the strip club while her brother Tony and Clay went inside.

Stepping inside, there were all kinds of freaks up in that joint. There were men with chicks, dancing with chicks who had dicks. She-males in dresses and tights, high as a kite. "What the fuck is going on up in here?" Clay asked. Eyes wide open looking around the club at the freak show in front of him. Tony just stared with his mouth hanging open just as shocked as Clay was.

Suddenly Tony heard a loud commotion and noticed his girls arguing with one of the She-males near the restroom. Running over to the restroom, Tony could see Nitty standing inside of the bathroom with his pants down to his ankles and his penis hanging out of his boxers. He was arguing with Mona and Kizz telling them to shut the door.

"Mind your mother fucking business bitch and shut this door before I fuck you up like I just did your friend." Nitty yelled as loud as he could for Kizz to close the bathroom door. Kizz didn't budge one bit holding the door open cursing Nitty out telling him how nasty he is. "You're a nasty mother fucker, hell no. You in here fucking a chick with a dick and you got the nerve to tell somebody to mind their business."

Kizz pulled out her camera phone and starting snapping pics of Nitty and his male chick. Tony skidded over to the bathroom and saw what the commotion was all about. "Nigga you are fucking chicks with dicks and got the nerve to put your hands on my sister. What the fuck. You want the best of both worlds don't you. Come here mother fucker."

Tony and Clay made their way into the bathroom and started beating the shit out of Nitty. They were kicking him in his ribs and punching him all up in his face. Tony punched him so many times that his hands was bloody. The transgender female who was inside of the bathroom sucking Nitty off, held on to her dress screaming as she ran out scared to death of the wrath that just flew in. "Yo! Fuck this shit. I'm about to kill this nasty mother fucker."

Tony pulled out his gun and cocked it while Nitty lay down on the bathroom floor crying like a little bitch. "Tony, no. Please Tony, don't kill him, I'm in love with him." Niema begged her brother not to shoot Nitty. Standing outside of the bathroom crying her eyes out. Tony looked at Niema and couldn't believe what he was hearing.

You going to let this dirty mother fucker beat on you and get caught letting another dude suck on his prick and you crying for me not to kill him. You know what Niema, I'm fucking done. Don't ever let me hear you say shit about this dirty ass nigga ever again. Tony placed his gun on safety and tucked it into his pants.

Let's get the fuck up out of here. Clay, Tony and The Clique moved quickly and headed back to the casino. "I should've killed that nigga. Who does shit like that and have a whole family at home waiting for them? That's that bullshit. He out here fucking around on some freaky shit and got his ass whipped. I don't want to hear nothing else about that fruit cake." "Whatever happens in Vegas stays in Vegas." Mona bussed out laughing along with everybody except for Niema.

The Clique jumped out of the elevator and ran to their room while Tony hurried up and opened the door. They quickly gathered up all their things and got the fuck out of dodge. Driving to the airport, Kizz called to book an emergency flight back to New York. "It looks like we stuck out here until the morning. Let's get a nice suite and crash until our flight arrives in the morning. It felt like old times.

Tony was sipping, his sister and the girls smoking their blunt and Clay sniffing lines of coke up in the suite they rented for the night before their flight. "Yo! Niema's man was in the bathroom fucking a man with a wig. I can't believe that shit." Tony chuckled. Still in shock about the night they just had. "It never fails, something is always popping off. I just can't catch a fucking break fuck it. It is what it is.

Clay interrupted Tony and started asking the girls personal questions on some truth or dare shit. "Have you ever fucked with any rich dudes Mona? I'm talking silver spoon type of dudes with legit businesses doctor's or lawyer's; you know the kind of men that they call sugar daddies, those white-collar pricks. Tony chuckled. Staring at Clay as he held onto his bill filled with cocaine.

It was two o'clock in the morning and Tony had a drop to make in a few hours after their flight back home with his man Clay before meeting up with Frederico. "Why did you ask me that Clay? I mean, yeah, I know a few doctors and lawyers. I had sexual relations and robbed at least three of them mother fuckers when my back was up against the wall.

These days all a doctor or lawyer can do for me is trick on me, help me get some pills and keep my people out of jail. I'm not trying to be booed up with a lawyer on some deep relationship shit. I'll be shook sitting around that mother fucker knowing damn well I just bagged up a kilo of coke right before I saw him. Mona at the table in the hotel giggling with her girls as Tony shook his head.

"See this is the type of shit I'm talking about. All the shit we say, know and do is thugged the fuck out. Anything other than this shit we are doing is foreign to us. I'm just trying to prove a point but this shit ain't getting nowhere." Clay put down his bill and continued talking. "Do you want to do this type of shit for the rest of your life?

This game is not built for us to be in it forever. After putting in all this work, I just feel like it's time to push up on bigger and better things. People, places and things will either make or break you. We don't have to stay in this situation forever. I'm trying make this money and move away and be free from all this bullshit. In this game you are constantly on the run or on point looking over your shoulder. You are never safe or at peace until you get out of the game.

You gotta know when to hold them and when to fold them and never trust anyone who is on the same paper trail; anybody can get popped when it comes to that money. Where I come from you gotta be on point with everything that you do. It's survival of the fittest. A woman can be the downfall or more dangerous than these dudes.

It's a dog eat dog world just keep your eyes open at all times." Clay mentioned. Picking up his bill of cocaine. "Clay was kicking some knowledge until he spit that downfall shit. No chicks in this room somebody's downfall. If anything, you might be the downfall, get the fuck out of here with that shit. Mona giggled. Looking at Clay like he was stupid. "Okay Mona, you got that one. I wasn't talking about you anyway slow down with all that gully shit."

Everybody laughed and enjoyed themselves for the night until the next morning. First thing in the morning Tony and his girls were sitting in the airport ready to board their flight back to New York City. The sun was shining bright and everyone was glad to get back home.

After the plane landed at LaGuardia Airport, Clay haled a cab and they all jumped in and headed to Mona's crib. Soon as they arrived at Mona's crib, she threw her luggage on the living room floor and headed straight for the bathroom. Vegas was crazy I had a good time especially winning at that slot machine. Kai mentioned. Waving the money, she won in the air dancing to the record playing on the radio.

"Yeah that shit was crazy seeing Nitty in that bathroom with his pants down. Tony chuckled. "Don't start Tony; bad enough I got to live with this shit knowing my ex-boyfriend is gay as hell." Niema rolled her eyes as Tony laughed thinking about Nitty getting his freak on. "I bet that mother fucker won't show his face for a minute. He damn sure embarrassed and got his ass whipped for putting his hands on you.

You should be glad to get rid of his fruity ass. I better not see you laying up with that nigga after this shit. Everyone in the room agreed with Tony as Clay went into the kitchen to make a phone call. Hey Tony, come here. Clay shouted. "It's a go with that Dynasty chick she is willing to catch a flight to Miami as soon as possible. "Ok my man, good looking say no more. Tony made the arrangements with Jimmy from Miami, had the money transferred into an account and set up a time and place where he could meet up with Princess and Dynasty.

Tony set up a meeting at one fish two fish out in Manhattan, so he could make the drop and send Dynasty, her sister and two of his goons to Miami with a kilo of cocaine. Walking into the seafood spot, the music was pumping through the jukebox playing that old school joint Remind Me.

"Patrice Rushen's voice is so pretty." Tony shouted. The vibe was groovy, and the lobster and crab legs filled up the whole spot. Clay looked around the restaurant and found Dynasty sitting in the cut with Princess. "Good evening ladies." Clay greeted the ladies as him and Tony sat down at the table. "So, I hear you want to do some business with two of my best girls. This is very risky for her to get on a flight with such a high quantity of coke. What is the rush? Why is it so important for this person to have my girls fly up so quick?" Princess asked. Looking into Tony's eyes full of passion. There's no rush Princess. A good friend of mines from Miami with a very lucrative business such as yourself, is on a time wave and he has the money to buy whatever he needs, so he paid for his services and I'm just here to deliver, give him what he paid for and make that happen.

Are you going to introduce me to your girl?" Tony asked. Staring at Dynasty. "Oh, pardon my manners. Dynasty this is Tony, he is affiliated and working with my father and I know you know Clay. Dynasty nodded her head. "Yes, I know Clay very well. "How are you gentlemen nice to meet you Tony I heard a lot about you in so little time. Dynasty mentioned taking off her sweater and placing it behind her chair. Her breasts were very voluptuous, and Clay could not stop staring at them. She had a Spanish accent with a caramel complexion. "I am willing to do the job for you. I must be paid up front. I was told that you will give me half before my flight and the other half as soon as the package is delivered am I correct." Dynasty looked at the gentlemen and waited for an answer.

"Yes, absolutely. What is the price to smuggle one kilo of coke?" Tony asked. Staring into Princess eyes. "Well I will let Dynasty tell you the price. She is very trust worthy and makes me very proud to work with her especially on jobs as great as this one." Princess looked at Dynasty and nodded her head for her to speak. "Well, I charge $10,000 for a half a kilo and $20,000 for a whole. My sister will accompany me on the flight and we both will smuggle the drugs to Miami.

We both will receive $5,000 apiece up front and the remainder soon as I confirm that the drop was successful. We are ready to fly out as soon as you make the arrangements." Dynasty was on point, ready to make it happen and waited on Tony so she could make moves. "Ok! I'm impressed. I have half of the money ready now.

Your flight leaves tomorrow in the morning. I received the picture of your sister's ID, so I know exactly who both of you are. I will have two of my goons accompany you both on the trip, so it looks like you all are traveling as a couple. Tony gave Dynasty $10,000, roundtrip plane tickets for both her and her sister and a kilo of cocaine. "My goons will have the location soon as you get off the plane.

She quickly placed everything into her purse and enjoyed a nice cocktail before she headed out of the restaurant with Princess. "Nice meeting you Tony. Dynasty whispered. Before shaking his hand. "It was a pleasure meeting you and seeing Princess again, you ladies are smart beautiful and gully. A lethal combination." The ladies laughed as Tony joked with them about their ways.

As Princes got up out of her seat, she grabbed her purse and proceeded to shake Clay and Tony's hand before leaving the restaurant. As Tony shook Princess's hand, he put $2,000 into her hands and said, thank you. Princess looked at Tony, passed him her card and told him to call her. "This is my private line. Give me a call whenever you like." Princess took the money, hugged Tony and headed out of the restaurant. Tony woke up with a lot on his mind.

He hadn't heard a word from Dynasty or his goons and it's been two days since he sent them over to Miami with the package. It was eight o'clock in the morning. The birds were chirping, the sun had already risen, and the phone was ringing off the hook. Tony looked at his phone to see Rico on the screen as his phone stopped ringing going to voicemail.

"Tony! Where are you? Soon as you get this message give me a call." Rico left his third message since last night. Tony was feeling a little pressure not knowing what the fuck to think. The money he lost from Beno robbing Mona put him in a fucked-up position. He had no choice but to call Rico to tell him exactly what happened. He thought about explaining everything and couldn't dial his number.

He decided to call Princess instead to find out where Dynasty was with Jimmy's package. "Hello, this is Princess please leave your name, number and a brief message and I will get back to you as soon as possible." "Hey, Princess hit me back. This is Tony. I am trying to get in touch with my goons and Dynasty and I haven't heard from them since they left for Miami.

As soon as Tony hung up the phone, he heard a knock at the door. Walking over to the door, the knocks and ringing of the doorbell repeated until he answered it. "Who is it? Tony asked. Cocking his gun quietly. "It's me Clay; open up the door. Opening the door, Tony was shocked to see Clay bleeding from a gunshot wound to his arm. "Tony, they shot me and took everything. I got robbed at gunpoint they took everything.

Two dudes dressed in all red, followed me from the gas station onto the Van Wyck while making a drop with the connect from Rockaway Blvd. I think it was a set up. Soon as I opened the door to my car, these niggas ran up on me and took everything I had in the back seat. They took my three kilos of coke and fifty thousand dollars.

I tussled with one of the niggas and tried to reach for my gun then he shot me in the arm and took off with the cash and the coke." Clay could hardly explain himself as the blood started gushing out of his arm. "We got to get you some help. Can't take you to the hospital because the cops will be all over us. I can take you to my man Caesar's house. His girl is a nurse. We can get that bullet out of you and get your arm cleaned and bandaged up come on."

Tony applied pressure to Clay's arm with a gauze then wrapped Clay's arm up with some adhesive bandages and rushed him over to his friend's crib. Tony helped Clay down the stairs once they reached Caesar's house. Caesar's wife had a table ready and prepared for Clay to lay on soon as he entered inside of the basement.

Clay was sweating losing a lot of blood and seemed very weak. "I'm going to need you to hold still. The nurse sterilized everything and put a warm rag over Clay's forehead. Then she began to clean the outside of the bullet wound. "Ok this is going to hurt a bit, you might want to drink this. Caesar passed Clay a bottle of Whiskey and told Clay to drink up. Clay guzzled the contents of the bottle and nodded his head at the nurse ready for her to pull the bullet out of his arm.

The nurse placed a sock into Clay's mouth, then she dug into his arm until she pulled the bullet out of him. The bullet made a clinging noise into the bowl. "Got it." Caesar smiled and kissed his wife as Clay looked at her still in pain but grateful she got the job done. "Thank you."

Clay mumbled.   As the nurse cleaned his wound once more and wrapped it up neatly. "You are more than welcome. I want you to take it easy on this arm. You don't want it to get infected. Right now, everything is fine, and your arm will heal in a few days. Leaving Caesar's house, Tony took Clay back over to Mona's crib, so they could get to the bottom of everything that's transpired and plan their next move. "This shit is getting ridiculous.

Who the fuck robbed you Clay? How the fuck are we going to explain all this shit to Rico? My mind is blown right now my man. Tony was fucked up in the head and couldn't put the pieces together, but he was ready to dig himself up out of the whole he was in.

"I spoke to Rico. He is a little upset about the cocaine, but he said that he had a job for the both of us and a way for us to repay him the moneys we lost." Clay mentioned. Barely speaking popping a pain killer into his mouth that he found in Mona's medicine cabinet. "What do you mean you spoke to Rico? When the fuck was this? I thought we both agreed not to let him no anything until we got the money back up.

Tony was a little confused, but he was also relieved to know that Rico was willing to work with him and give him a chance to make good of the mess he made. Ok so I suppose you were going to tell me about Rico before or after you got shot. Tony looked at Clay with the side eye waiting for him to explain himself. "I had to call Rico or we both would have the mob running up in here right now looking for us.

This shit is deep and the only way we are going to make good is to do this next job. First thing in the morning we are going to meet Rico at his restaurant and square everything out. For now, I need to get some rest, so I can clear my fucking head. Clay rested on the blankets Tony set out for him and let the meds work on his pain while he tried to get some sleep.

While Clay slept, Tony took a hot shower and got himself a little rest, so he'd be ready for whatever Rico had planned for him. The following morning, Tony and Clay met up with Rico to see what he wanted them to do for him. "Hello my friends. This is a pleasant surprise. I thought you two wouldn't show up after the fiasco you both caused. Clay and Tony didn't respond with words. They just looked at Rico ready for his plan to make everything even.

"There is a very lovely girl I met. Her name is Annessa. She has the best head in the world. I love it especially when she wears those cute little glasses." Rico smiled as he continued. "I met Annessa at National Savings Bank. She helped me out with an account before I took her out to lunch. She's been very generous with me helping me launder money back and forth from business to business like my friend Mr. Roberts before he passed away. I pay her incredibly good to keep my business accounts in good standing.

This bank she works at has a vault with three million dollars inside. At exactly 10AM sharp, Annessa will be sitting there at the bank waiting for you to come inside. Your next job is to rob the bank and bring the money to this location."

Rico passed Tony an address to where he wants him to go after they leave the bank job. "I will send a car to pick you up in the alley at the side entrance. If anything goes wrong, you never met me, and we never spoke of this job. I already explained everything to Clay the night before. He is aware of everything that you need to know in case you have any questions. I expect to see you at the location with the money by 11:30am.

There is a blue van waiting outside with tinted windows. I wish you both the best of luck and I will see you both soon enough." Tony couldn't believe his ears. He looked at Rico and nodded his head to everything he just told him. Leaving the restaurant, both men looked at each other and kept walking until they reached the van.

"You mean to tell me we about to rob a bank. This is the type of shit I'm talking about. He should have been put me on to do some shit like this. We don't have any masks; what kind of shit is that? I'm about to rob the shit out of that bank." Tony took out his gun waving it around in the air. "Yo! Put that gun down. Are you crazy?" Clay looked around to see if anyone saw them as he drove the van.

"Relax. I know what I'm doing. I've been doing this shit since I was two." Tony laughed. Putting the gun back at his side. "Listen, let's just run in there, do what we gotta do and get the fuck up out of there. Frederico got a few men coming through for us as we speak. There is a teller who works there named Annessa. She's going to be behind the window at the front desk.

She sits directly near the vault with all the cash. Once we get inside, there's no turning back. Make sure you keep your eyes open at all times." Clay explained the measures of the bank job inside of a dark blue van with tinted windows to his man Tony and two other assailants before heading inside to rob it. "Look, it's about to be a hostage situation if anything goes left. I'm not going back to jail.

I'm not going back to the pen. I'd rather die than to go back. If anything happens in there, I'm going all out. It's kill or be killed fuck that." Tony let his partner know that he was down for whatever and he was ready to get rich or die trying. Walking into the bank, there were three different tellers with a few people standing in each line.

Standing on the line, Tony looked up and noticed two cameras pointed in the direction of the entrance near the security guard. He had on a pair of shades and a black hoodie and had a black stocking cap up under his hoodie ready to set shit off. He quickly looked around the bank and noticed the teller that his man described inside of the van before they walked in. Annessa was sitting at the front desk talking to a potential customer like she said she would be.

She knew everything that was about to go down and agreed to play along with the robbery taken place. She disclosed all info of the security guards who were on shift that morning. She also had complete access to all camera recordings and shut them off for the day. Annessa gave a full and accurate description of each vault that had money in it.

She also included the time of one of the security guards thirty-minute break and the exact time he usually returned into the bank. Tony's partner Clay watched him from a distance as he stood on the line; then he signaled him to make his move as he walked up to the teller. "Welcome to National Saving Bank. How may I help you?" The teller greeted the gentleman who stood before her on the line. Tony approached her in full speed placing a pistol into her face.

"Don't you move bitch, or I'll blow your mother fucking head off." The bank teller was frightened as she listened to everything the gunman asked of her. "Everybody get on the fucking floor now." Tony shouted. Waving his gun in the air. "Listen up this is a bank robbery.

We are robbing this bank. Now you can comply and live or you can resist and die. The choice is yours. I suggest you comply comfortably, so you can get back home to your families safely. The four gunmen were robbing the bank in broad day light. "We got about six minutes to empty out the vaults." Pointing his gun at the teller who sat on the floor near the front desk. One of the teller's behind the window, placed her hand on the button to signal the silent alarm. "I said don't move, stupid mother fucker." Clay walked up to the teller and smacked her in the face with the butt of his gun. The loud cries rang throughout the bank as the teller sobbed in agony; bloody faced and hurt by the blow to her head. The security guard who lay on the floor thought of reaching for his pistol as the tellers leaned against the wall on the floor while Tony tied their hands and feet up behind the counter.

"Not so fast." Clay whispered. Grabbing the gun out of the security guards hand. The silent alarm that the teller pressed, alerted the National Police Station. "We got a possible robbery attempt at National Savings Bank. I repeat, we have a possible robbery attempt at National Savings Bank. I need two units down there right now." The dispatcher at the police department alerted the police officers on duty and gave them the location of the robbery. "Please don't kill us. You can take whatever you want. I have a family at home. I have two daughters who are waiting for me to pick them up from school." The Caucasian woman pleaded with the robber begging him not to take the lives of her and her co-workers. "Put the money in the bag and shut the fuck up. You think I give a fuck about you and your family right now? Say another word and I will blow your head off.

Tony looked at the lady who was crying with disgust. All gunmen had four large bags filled with cash. Tony proceeded to the next vault to retrieve more money. "Come on that's enough. Don't be greedy. That's enough let's go." Clay hollered. Pointing the gun at the customers lying on the floor. Tony ignored every word and proceeded to take more money filling up a fifth bag. As Tony filled the bag, he could hear the loud sirens approaching the bank.

"Come on we got to get the fuck out of here right now." Looking out the window, Clay could see two police cars in front of the bank. He quickly grabbed one of the tellers who worked at the bank and demanded her to escort him and his crew to another exit.

Running through the bank, Clay grabbed the woman's hair swinging her body as they made a run from the police. The teller pointed to the exit and cried covering her face with her hands. Clay shoved the woman to the floor and proceeded to open the door. "Freeze! Don't move mother fucker. The police officer shouted. Standing in the back exit of the bank pointing a pistol at Clay's face.

Both gunmen looked at one another and put their hands in the air. Tony was in shock looking at the police officer standing in front of him. The police officer removed each bag of money from the robbers and placed it inside of a black Suburban truck with tinted windows.

He then placed Tony, Clay and the third assailant inside of the truck and closed the door. Tony and Clay were confused as to why the fourth assailant who was with them didn't get into the car. As the officer closed the door. He dropped the fifth bag of money and shot the fourth assailant in the head. He then nodded to his partner who stayed at the scene of the crime waiting for back up while pulling off in the Suburban.

"What the fuck is going on? He just killed my man right in front of us." Clay screamed from the back of the truck. Tony attempted to open the door, but it was locked from the inside. The police officer pulls up to the Ramada Inn and got out of the car. He then walked over to another Suburban and hopped inside.

Tony and Clay were bugging in the back seat trying their best to open the back door. Suddenly Rico jumps out of the Suburban and walks over to the truck where Tony and Clay were in the parking lot. "Hello my friends. I would like you to meet officer Fernandez. Rico and the officer jumped into the truck. The officer shook the hand of Tony and Clay and the third assailant. We will be doing a lot of business together. The job you just pulled off was incredible.

Everything you lost, has been forgiven. We are back in business and we will start fresh on a clean slate. I want you to take the gray Suburban and meet me at my ranch out in Long Island. I will be right behind you. Rico then placed the large bags of money inside of the gray truck. He filled up a duffle bag full of money and gave it to the officer.

The officer then went inside of the hotel and put the money he just received from Rico into a room. When the officer returned, he shook Rico's hand and waved before he got back into the black Suburban and pulled off. Once the officer returned to the scene of the crime, his partner had already explained how the other assailants got away and fled in a red sedan leaving one behind who got into a shootout with the two officers before they shot him in the head.

Driving to Long Island, Clay and Tony were ecstatic screaming and hollering, waving their guns up in the air. "We did that shit. We got all this fucking money. My man Rico came through with the mother fucking police. That shit was gully." Tony shouted. Driving and smiling in the getaway car.

Tony and Clay got away with three million in cash, gave Rico a million and split the rest of the money three ways. Every dime that was lost from the stolen kilos, was paid in full. After Rico, Tony and Clay counted the money, they celebrated big time and partied at his ranch with plenty stripper's, booze and coke. Tony and Clay stashed their moneys in a safe place laid low for a minute and focused on not attracting any unnecessary attention. Rico had dirty cops on the payroll and everything was smooth like butter.

CHAPTER 10

The Cookout

The grass was green on Tony's side of town. He bought a nice house out in Long Island and set up a few businesses with Clay and Rico. Shit was falling into place on many levels for the kid. Tony came a long way and paid a long debt to society. He did a lot of dirt throughout his lifetime, but he's now ready to make everything right with himself, friends and family. He opened a Big Brother and Big Sister camp for the youth where hundreds of young children and teenagers benefit from the program each year.

The facilities are available to the community and school groups that focused on bettering the lives of the youth with after school programs, summer vacations, holiday giveaways, food and clothing drives. Living in the fast life has taught Tony many lessons along the way.

Criminal minded activities were the norm for Tony as a youngster and this time around; he decided to clean up his life and give back as much as he has taken from his own community. He opens up to the children telling them his many crazy stories and teaches them right from wrong and explains to the children that they have a choice in life. He wants to be able to provide some hope and give the youth a better example than he was given when he grew up in the hood. In life you can either go one way or the other.

There are many chances to get on the right track and there are many chances lost by refusing to make a change for the better. Growing up in the hood as a young child living in the projects; you are faced with many obstacles and subjected to a lot of things that you have no control of. Drugs were a big part of Tony's childhood. Everything that he did, he was taught to do and did it with a smile because that was all he knew. Now that he has a better perspective, he is ready and willing to make a difference in kids' lives who are living in the same predicament. The streets don't love nobody.

It may look good to have all the fly clothes, drive in the hottest cars and sell drugs to the people you grew up with. That life will never have a perfect ending. There will always be consequences to every bad choice you make.

Whether you get caught by the law or fall victim to addictive drugs or simply die by the gun. If you have a strong heart, you can get through any obstacle in life. The choice is always yours to take a stand for your own life and pave a better way. If you choose to do better, you will get better. If you choose to live a life in the streets; be prepared to receive the belly of the beast. Being with The Clique has always put a smile on Tony's face. He was so happy to be able to walk away from a lot of fucked up shit.

"We got Mac and cheese, collard greens, turkey wings, potato salad, barbecue ribs, fried and baked chicken, lobster and shrimp, drinks you name it. Mona and her girls set up shop at Tony's home.

They were having a great big cookout celebrating life and enjoying one another's company for a change. After Tony came up with Rico and Clay during the heist, he gave all the girls in The Clique a lump sum of money to start their own businesses. Mona had always dreamed of owning a restaurant, so she went to culinary school to get a license to cook and open up a fabulous restaurant when the right time approaches.

She also continued to write novels and is doing very well with her own publishing company. Mona loves every aspect of her life right or wrong because every experience has made her a strong individual and has taught her lessons that you can never learn at any school. The body count they all have witnessed were by the dozens. Mona managed to build her self-esteem and live a productive life.

Her sister Kai held on to her beauty supply store and went back to college to receive her master's degree. Kizz remained working as a Correctional Officer and chose to give her life to the lord. It was a hard road to travel but she was focused on bettering her ways and living life legit this time around. Vince was still facing life in prison and was content knowing that his kids were making better choices and moving forward with their lives. Tony paid a visit to see him every month and kept him living easy from the inside.

Kema got her children back and made peace with her mother. She's doing very well in life. She started making and selling vintage clothing at her own boutique out in the village; making life beautiful the way it supposed to be.

No one in life is ever perfect and we all for short and make many mistakes from time to time. The goal is to stop repeating the same mistakes. Kema was good with knowing that and took every little step one day at a time. Niema finally left that cheating no good man of hers.

She broke off all connections with Nitty and started a new life for herself and her child. No matter what your situation is in life; if a man treats you like shit, leave him like a bad habit. Absolutely no one is worth your peace, your smile or your self-esteem. Dick comes a dime a dozen. You can even buy a plastic one that'll give you some act right. It is not that serious. Learn how to love yourself first, get your life together, teach your kids that you are worthy of better things and make it happen.

You are the only person who can make your life better. No one else can ever face your hurdles of responsibility. The Cook Out was popping. Rico arrived with all his people. He even brought a few dirty cops to party at Tony's house. Ever since the heist, Rico knew he could finally trust Clay and Tony.

After setting Clay up for that robbery, he's now learning to use better judgement. Burgers and sausages were cooking on the grill and the food was set up with plenty drinks on deck. Tony danced to the beat as he watched everyone smiling and laughing enjoying themselves. It felt good as hell to be on the other side of the game. He spent many years dreaming of days like this and he refused to go backwards. The dancer Dynasty that worked for Princess was found dead in Miami Beach.

She never made the drop and ran into some dealers in which she tried selling the kilo of cocaine and got herself killed. Her sister is still out in Miami dancing and stripping on the run. Tony's goons got home safely after one big goose chase looking for Dynasty after she got away from them at the airport. They were out in Miami for two weeks looking for her until they found out she was shot and killed.

She made a pretty bad choice by going out there thinking she was going to get away with selling someone else's product. The cards just didn't end well in her favor. Beno found out his brother was murdered when they found his remains out in New Jersey Shore. He went crazy and got himself admitted into a Psychiatric mental institution.

The ship sailed far away, and he is knee deep stuck in a world of hallucination. After he robbed Mona for those kilos of coke, he was on the hideout thinking that Tony was looking for him. When he heard of his brother's murder; that was all she wrote. He started using most of the coke he stole and ended up addicted running the streets talking to himself and acting coocoo for cocaine.

When you in these streets you never know the hand your dealt. You just gotta play your cards right. It's a cold world out there and karma is a real bitch. Kai's phone rang while she was serving a plate to one of the guests at the barbecue. "Hello. Kai answered. "Hello Kai. I'm a friend of the family and I just wanted to call and inform you of Waynie's murder.

He was found dead on 42nd street in front of a peep show. The intensity of his murder is just ludicrous. Sorry to inform you of such news. I was with him the night he was robbed and beat. I managed to get away from the situation because they told me to mind my fucking business. Unfortunately, Waynie must have had an enemy who wanted him to suffer. "Oh, my goodness. Waynie's friend just called my phone and told me that he was killed.

He found my number in his phone along with a few other family members and wanted to inform us of the situation. He was found on 42nd street. He also told me that Waynie was beat badly and left for dead with his penis in his mouth. Who the hell would do such a thing? What the fuck?" Kai ran to the bar to make herself a strong drink.

Mona just looked at her sister, poured out a little liquor and kept on dancing to the music. You don't have too many feelings for a pervert who molests little girls. Can't blame or knock anyone for acting cold towards the person who violated their body and mind as a child, leaving emotional scars to carry for a lifetime. Rest in peace. Mona mumbled. Sipping on a Pina Colada.

Everyone at the barbecue started the electric slide, laughing and joking and smoking and having a ball. The weather was a cool breeze, and everyone was content at ease. You gotta take the good with the bad and within the good and bad; you gotta be able to own up to the shit that you do and learn from your faults and mistakes in life.

This world holds a lot of skeletons and secrets and many stories will never be told because some people are so used to pushing shit under the rug; living in a house of lies. Constantly throwing stones when they live in glass houses.

The truth shall set you free and the goal is to be true to yourself. You might be able to fool others, but you will never fool the reflection in the mirror. Tony stood in his backyard with his chef hat on turning the burgers and sausages on the grill. *"That mother fucker Waynie got exactly what he deserved. He will never hurt another child again. Rest in peace bitch."* Tony waited ten years to pay the nigga back who hurt his best friend.

He will take that secret with him to his grave. As the old folks might say; what you don't know won't hurt you. In this case they were one hundred percent correct.

In this game you've got to be a good hustler whether it's book or street smarts. If you got the fire in you to submerge, you can become anything you want in life. No matter if your scarred, no matter if your battered, no matter if your addicted to drugs, no matter if you did a long sentence in the penitentiary.

The life you lead will always be yours no matter how many times you fuck up, but you can never win if you ain't right within. Take care of yourself mentally as well as physically. Keep your mind right and rebuild yourself every day you wake. There will be people who will never like you because you love yourself. Stand up for what you believe in, even if it means standing alone. Princess came through and brought her strippers along to party.

Her and Mona finally got the chance to meet and they actually got along really well. Princess tried to pursue Tony every chance she got, but Mona cock blocked every occasion. Tony had the woman on a love jones and he was enjoying the ride. Princess kept all of her connects and she's running a slew of businesses. The game kept rolling in the doe in many places with different faces. The Clique and Tony partied until sunrise happy to be together as a family. They stood by one another through thick and thin and they would do it all over again if they had to. In a world full of lessons, life is your teacher. Laugh love learn live life and never be ashamed of your story you might save someone's life…

THE END...

FIND ME

Author/Publisher- Toylin Simone

Toyco Publishing LLC

toycoworld@gmail.com

Atlanta Georgia

FaceBook- Toylin Simone

Instagram- @Toyco